JOEY

Gates of Heaven – Book 4

M. Tasia

ALSO BY M. TASIA

The Boys of Brighton series

Gabe

Sam's Soldiers

Rick's Bear

Jesse

Coop

Travis

Grady

Vincent

Shadow

The Holidays

The Gates of Heaven series

Saint

Finn

James

EVERYONE LOVES THE BOYS OF BRIGHTON

"I loved this book and I love this town. I hope there's going to be more."
—Melissa Lemons on *Gabe*

"An amazing read that was filled with lust, love, crazy hot sex, danger, action and so much more This is the first book I have read in this series but I will definitely be reading more in the future."
—Gay Book Reviews on *Sam's Soldiers*

"I was crazy impressed that the author made me teary over the ending of a relationship that I shouldn't have even been invested in. I didn't yet know these characters yet the author made me hurt for them. That takes some mad writing skills!"
—Love Bytes Reviews

"Jesse and Royce together have my heart. Jesse has it all by himself."
—The Book Junkie Reads on *Jesse*

"So much action, intrigue, drama and angst for the long awaited story of Grady and Ben. This was worth the wait. Sexy and sweet. I can't wait for the next."
—SamD on *Grady*

"I knew this one would be my favorite to date! There was something about Vincent that said awesome then came Tristan."
—Booky on *Vincent*

"This installment of the Boys of Brighton was so good! I loved Shadow and Randy 's story I was hooked from the first page to the last. This book was definitely worth the wait!"
—AG on *Shadow*

"I have loved this series from the very first story and this holiday novella is simply perfect. We get a glimpse of all our couples and what is happening in their lives while the holidays explode around them. I cannot wait for more!"
—bookobsessed on *The Holidays*

EVERYONE'S NEWEST LOVE – THE GATES OF HEAVEN

"Having read the entire Boys of Brighton series, I was eagerly awaiting Saint's story and it was so worth the wait. I enjoyed every word. I am always amazed by authors that bring characters to life so much that you can hardly wait for the next story. Cannot wait for

Finn and Miguel to have their turn. While I'm waiting I'll reread the Boys of Brighton series!" —Debbie Kay on *Saint*

"Ms. Tasia has done it again! This is Saint's story, for readers of the Brighton Boys, you'll know he needs a break! After being forced to become a plastic surgeon by his father, he rebels by assisting people in 3rd world countries, which puts him in the position to be kidnapped and tortured. You really feel for him, that's for sure! Max is the perfect man for poor Saint's battered soul, not that he doesn't have his own issues! Overall, this was engaging, steady paced and chock full of all the feels!" —Avid Reader on *Saint*

"Finn and Miguel stole my heart. This is a great Sunday afternoon read. Finn's character jumped off the page as his story developed through each chapter. I loved reading his truth and watching him and Miguel find their home in each other." —K.A. Brown on *Finn*

"Another tale from the Gates of Heaven, another two brilliant MCs we get to know very well. I loved both the plot and the characters, all their emotions and insecurities on full display. All the descriptions and world building were very vivid, providing a great background for an emotional story of self discovery and developing attraction." —AL on *Finn*

"James...what can I say. I couldn't put it down. This is my first book in the series, so it definitely can be read and enjoyed as a standalone, but it will not be my last. Now I'm going to read the previous stories. Solid writing with a gripping style, characters that are right up my alley, and the kind of chemistry I love in my romances. What more do you need for a great reading experience." —cinnamon on *James*

"This is really a great series and I def recommend it. I loved James and Ross, it was a rough start for the two, but they worked it out. I can't wait for more, love everything M. TASIA writes!" — TammyKay on *James*

www.BOROUGHSPUBLISHINGGROUP.com

PUBLISHER'S NOTE: This is a work of fiction. Names, characters, places and incidents either are the product of the author's imagination or are used fictitiously. Any resemblance to actual events, locales, business establishments or persons, living or dead, is coincidental. Boroughs Publishing Group does not have any control over and does not assume responsibility for author or third-party websites, blogs or critiques or their content.

JOEY
Copyright © 2020 M. Tasia

ISBN 978-1-951055-52-3

This has been possible because of the love and support of my family. Love you Craig, Samantha, Katie, and Jason.

ACKNOWLEDGMENTS

Thank you to my amazing publisher for taking the time to play tour guide in her diverse and stunning area of Southern California. Your indomitable spirit and strength inspires me to continue to grow as an author. Also, to my sisters-in-law, thank you for coming along and supporting my dream. The love and strength of family is the cornerstone of my career.

JOEY

Prologue

Joey wiped down the bar as he watched the party get under way. Detective Ross was still recovering from his gunshot wound, but it had been over a month since he'd been released from the hospital. Each time Joey had seen the detective, he'd looked better than the time before.

Joey had been working at The Gates as a bartender for the last six months, and he loved his job. The bosses were honest and fair. The rest of the staff seemed to be working out fine, and Marian had taken Joey under her wing.

"Hey, Joey, can I have that bottle of champagne for Ross, please?" Finn asked from the other end of the bar.

"Sure, boss. I can bring it over to the table along with glasses if you'd like. Oh, and I'll bring some sparkling apple juice for Becca." Joey tilted his neck back. He had to look up at most people who worked at The Gates. With him being five foot five, it felt like he had a permanent crick.

"You're an angel. You think of all the scenarios. Thank you," Finn praised before walking back to his group of friends.

There were people in suits, police officers popping in and out to give their best wishes, and a group that looked better suited to the country than the city. The whole bunch was happy to have Ross still living in the world beside them.

He couldn't blame any one of them. Ross had always been a straight-up guy. Treated people with respect and had always said hello to Joey when the detective came to The Gates.

Joey couldn't help but be a little bit jealous, and he felt horrible for it. He couldn't think of a single person who would do the same for him. Especially if they found out what's wrong with him, and who he really was, or more to the point, his family lineage.

That was why he began bartending. It was the perfect job. No one really noticed the person slinging drinks. Customers would talk about their lives and their woes to their heart's content, and not one had asked Joey about himself.

Well, maybe the bosses, but they were running the place and needed the information when he was hired. Joey had given them the bare minimum, but they never pried deeper than the initial background screening, and since he wasn't really who he said he was , it was all good. He'd felt terrible deceiving them, especially since they'd made it clear that they were there for him if he needed them.

But he'd changed his name for that exact reason: anonymity and acceptance. Joey was not part of the life his family had forged and stolen. Never had been and never would be. He'd sworn it standing over his mother on her deathbed, and he would sooner die before breaking that oath.

Joey wrapped the bottle of Dom Perignon with a starched white napkin then placed it in the standing ice bucket. On a tray, he put sparkling apple juice and half a dozen champagne flutes and then headed over to the tables. He never thought to uncork the champagne. Typically, one of the guests wanted to do it, and frequently enjoyed the show of the cork popping out with a distinctive noise.

The restaurant had been shut down for the occasion, which Joey didn't mind. It would be a quiet shift before he had to go home. He pushed down that sick feeling he often got at the thought of returning to his empty, shoebox-size apartment.

"Ah, here we go. It's not a celebration without champagne," Saint announced as Joey set the bucket alongside the table, then took the glasses and apple juice off the tray and placed them on the table.

"Do you mind opening that for us, Joey?" Finn, his other boss, asked.

"I thought you might like the honor, boss," Joey suggested.

"You're a part of The Gates crew, have at it. Did you bring yourself a glass?" Saint was always so generous.

"No, sir." Joey could feel the warmth of acceptance seeping into his sore bones.

"Well, let's open that up, and then you go grab yourself a glass," Finn said.

The smaller boss was terrific. He never gave out orders unless it was for your own good, and typically, Joey didn't catch on until after the fact. Joey liked and respected Finn, and worked twice as hard to please him.

"Yes, sir," Joey agreed. The bosses used to try to get him to call them by their first names, but he'd refused, and, thankfully, they stopped trying. His mother taught him to respect those who worked hard and made a good and honest life for themselves.

Joey removed the foil and muselet from around the top of the bottle and cork. He wrapped a cloth around the top of the bottle and began pulling while he turned the cork. He could feel their stares, which made him shake a little. However, it must have been enough to lose control of the cork, sending it about ten feet across the room and straight into the head of one of Ross's fellow police officers.

Joey stood frozen to the spot, his heart beating frantically. "I'm so sorry." Holy shit. He'd ruined the party. Now the cops would notice him, look into his past, and he'd be fired. Yep, he was paranoid.

After a few agonizing moments, Ross broke out laughing. "That'll teach you to keep your eyes open, Webb."

Officer Webb laughed, and so did the rest of the people in the room. Thank God. Joey quickly set the bottle down.

"I'll get you some ice for your head."

He raced back to the safety of his bar, grabbed a plastic bag, and filled it with crushed ice. When he turned around, he found Officer Webb had followed him and was now standing on the other side of the bar with a glass of champagne in his hand.

Joey wrapped the bag of ice in a clean towel and handed it to his victim. "I'm truly sorry. I don't know what happened." Of course, he knew what happened. He'd been the center of attention and lost his shit, once again.

The officer smiled, which lit up his entire face. "Call me Sam, and don't worry about it, accidents happen. This is for you." Webb handed him the glass of champagne

"I was nervous." *Why did I say that?*

"I could tell. I'm guessing you don't like standing out." Sam's deep voice could melt butter, which made Joey even more nervous.

Was he that obvious? "No. I'd rather stay back."

"Someone as handsome as you in the background, that might be near impossible and a damned shame," Officer Webb said. "Thanks to your lucky shot, it's given me a reason to talk to you."

Joey could feel his cheeks warming, and he knew he was blushing. *I'm such a child.* His birth certificate might say he was twenty-eight, but his stature led people to believe he had barely broken eighteen.

Sam took the ice pack and held it to the side of his head before reaching into his freshly pressed navy shirt pocket.

"I'll let you make it up to me," he said, then placed his business card on the polished bar top. "Let me take you out for coffee sometime, and we'll call it even."

"How is that making it up to you if you're the one paying for the coffee?" Joey asked.

Sam smiled, and Joey could feel his heart speeding up once again. "Because you'll save me from drinking my coffee all alone. Think about it." Sam winked and turned to rejoin the party.

Had Officer Webb asked him out on a date? Wouldn't that send dear old Granddad Bishop into convulsions? Joey tucked the card into his pants' pocket, poured the champagne down the sink, and went back to cleaning the bar.

He sure as certain was interested, but that coffee rendezvous could never happen. Joey had to keep his secrets safe, and dating a cop was the absolute wrong thing to do to assure that continued to happen.

Besides, Joey's days were numbered anyway.

But, as his mom used to say, there was no harm in dreaming.

Chapter One

Joey placed the glass tumbler on the bar counter, dropped in a sugar cube, a dash of bitters, a lemon twist, and a touch of water before grabbing his pestle and muddling the ingredients into a paste. Next, he grabbed the whiskey and poured out two ounces, filled the tumbler with ice, another splash of water, and stirred it well before adding an orange slice and a maraschino cherry.

He took the cocktail and napkin over to the end of the bar and set it down in front of an older man who'd been coming in five days a week at eight in the evening ever since Joey had begun tending bar here.

"Here's your old fashioned, Mr. Kennedy," Joey said. "Hope you're not still in the doghouse with Mrs. Kennedy?"

"You know, son, I should move in there full time at this rate," he grumbled good-naturedly before picking up his drink and taking a sip. "Ah, now that's a proper drink."

"Thank you, sir," Joey acknowledged before grabbing his cloth and wiping the stray water droplets off the polished wood bar top. "Call me if you need a menu."

Mr. Kennedy raised his glass in salute and went back to his *LA Times*. Joey glanced around the lounge, checking on each of his remaining five guests. Though still early in the evening, his shift was coming to an end.

As he typically did, Joey had offered to stay until closing, but Saint had already allowed him to stay late three days this week, so the answer had understandably been *no*.

Along with the *no* came a healthy dose of concern from the bosses. Finn had always been kind to Joey, and so had Saint, the owner, for that matter. However, only Finn seemed to have the ability to see straight through him. As if he knew what Joey was thinking. Which was terrifying, if it'd been really true.

Finn had stated, and not for the first time, that he worried Joey was overworking himself. Considering he'd already racked up over fifty-two hours this week, and still had another shift to go, Joey could see his point. Joey's fatigue was weighing on him, sure, but not more than it usually did, at least not enough to stop him from working and getting the OT. He wasn't sure how to explain to the bosses that The Gates had become his safe place. The place Joey felt the best and most comfortable. Plus, he needed the money.

It didn't matter, and he doubted anyone, other than the bosses, even cared where he was and what he was doing. Getting ready to wrap it up for the night, he went to restock the coolers, cut up a few more lemon wedges, and wash down his work area.

The intricately carved wood panels mounted behind the bar had always attracted him, and he'd find himself staring at them. Joey would often wonder if the winding staircase and the gates depicted held a special meaning other than for the name of the building.

After one final walk around the lounge to check on his guests, Joey returned to his paperwork so that he could cash out when Brad arrived for his evening shift. Joey would do his official count in the office after he was relieved. He picked up his travel water bottle and downed the contents. He'd have to remember to refill it before he walked to his apartment.

Ten minutes later, Brad arrived and took over. Joey's hope that his replacement would call in sick wasn't realized. He hadn't wanted the other man to become ill, but he'd wanted to stay where he felt safe. Protected. Brad was a nice enough guy, but the way his gaze shifted around each area of the bar reminded Joey of how he'd been taught by his dear old granddad to case a joint.

With that in mind, he'd decided to keep an eye on the guy in case Brad had motives involving more than a paycheck.

Joey stopped to say good night to Mr. Kennedy and then took his receipts to the office before clocking out. Everything was computerized, and most people had their receipts emailed to them, but a few die-hards paid in cash, or wanted a paper trail. Joey opened the office door to a familiar sight: Saint in the arms of his boyfriend, Max. The two behaved like lovesick teenagers, which was beautiful and saddening at the same time. Beautiful, to see two people completely in love, and saddening because nothing that great wasn't ever going to happen to him.

The moment the two realized they weren't alone anymore, they broke apart, and Saint went from leaning against his desk to sitting behind it.

"Sorry, I should have knocked first," Joey was quick to say.

Max began laughing, and Saint's cheeks turned red, as they always did when the two were caught in one of their clenches.

"Don't be sorry. We're the ones who should be able to control ourselves," Saint said while staring straight at Max, who was grinning from ear to ear.

"Don't, it gives guys like me hope," Joey teased to make sure that they knew he wasn't offended. "Promise me, if clothes are about to come off, you two go back into the hub, or you might blind these virgin baby blues of mine."

All three laughed as he'd hoped, and with that accomplished, Joey headed to the corner desk reserved for staff. As always, he organized the receipts by timestamp, and put them in the tray with his name. Then he flipped up the laptop, logged in, and checked out for the night.

One bright spot that had brought a bit of calm into Joey's day was that he'd made enough in tips by three o'clock to cover the last bit of his rent, which took a lot of weight off his sore shoulders.

The minimum wage in LA was higher than almost anywhere since they had a living wage, and Gates employees were paid over the living wage. The problem was Joey's health plan had a high deductible, and he had medical bills up the wazoo. He figured he'd be paying off his portion of those services well into his fifties, if he made it that far. Plus, certain medications he had to take weren't covered in the plan's formulary, but they were essential to keeping him healthy enough to pay the hefty medical bills.

"So, how are things?" Max asked as he came to sit in the chair on the other side of the staff desk. The boss's boyfriend had always watched Joey closely, and he was unsure why, but close scrutiny of any kind made Joey nervous.

He'd been so deep in sorting out his bills in his head, he hadn't noticed Max walking over to the desk. Joey knew better, and he had to stay more vigilant about his surroundings. "Good, sir."

"I'm not one of your bosses or a customer. Call me Max."

"Okay, Max, things are good."

"Great to hear, and how did the coffee date with Officer Webb go last week?" Max asked as subtly as a freight train barreling through a brick wall.

Joey was caught off guard. He'd been trying to forget that it had ever happened and not for the reasons anyone would think. Yeah, he'd broken down and given in during a weak, lonely moment and had accepted Sam's invitation. They'd met at the coffee shop a few blocks away from The Gates. Sam was funny and attentive, not to mention a classic TDH who looked like he should be on the cover of GQ.

Joey had known before he'd walked into the busy coffee shop that he was in trouble, Sam was out of his league, and that Joey had no business being there. Sam stood when Joey approached the the corner table, and pulled out Joey's chair, waiting until he sat before Sam retook his seat. Joey ordered a double-double cappuccino, which was all he could afford, and before he could protest, Sam added muffins and pastries, chiding Joey that he looked pale, and then Sam paid for everything before Joey could even protest.

Joey had been concerned the two of them would have nothing to talk about. Sam was a cop and Joey was born into a family who lived on the other side of the law. However, as it turned out, they couldn't shut up.

"You seem to enjoy being a bartender," Sam said as he slathered jelly on his scone.

Joey nodded, swallowing his gulp of coffee. "It's a great way to meet all kinds of people, and the more they drink, the looser their tongues. I've heard all kinds of stories."

Sam chuckled. "I bet you have. Which is your favorite so far?"

Joey had heard everything from cheating and broken relationships to promotions, graduations, first babies, and the thrill of new love. He didn't want to share anything hinting at love or a relationship with Sam. Bad enough Joey sat there trying not to stare moon-eyed at Sam's incredible cheekbones and puffy lips.

"I have a few, but this one's funny." Sam sat back waiting for Joey to continue. "A group of five girls came in to celebrate their friend's twenty-first birthday. She was the youngest of the group and this was her first legal drink. They sat at the bar since all the round tops were taken, and pulled out those little pointy hats like kids wear at parties. After they stuck the hats on their heads, they ordered lemon drop martinis all around. When I put the drinks in front of them, the birthday girl held up hers and twirled the glass, staring at the bottom. When one of her friends asked her what she was doing, she said she was looking for the lemon drop. Before I had a chance to tell her the lemon liqueur was in the drink, the girls broke up laughing. I didn't know lemon drops were a candy, they had to explain to her that there wasn't candy in the drink, and explain to me what lemon drop candies looked like. We were all laughing so hard, Saint came over, and one of the girls took one look at him and shouted he was her dream man and that he had to father her children."

Sam laughed, and shook his head.

"Right?" Joey continued. "When Saint told her he was taken, I thought she was going to cry. Then Max came over and another girl shouted, 'I'll take him' and we all cracked up, even Saint. Max looked at Saint and asked, 'What's so funny, babe?' and all the girls gasped then pretended they were sobbing because Max and Saint were off the market, and because they were really unavailable to the girls."

Sam's smile was a thing to behold. His face lit up, and his eyes danced. "Great story. I'm going to have to razz Saint and Max."

Joey waved his hand frantically. "Don't you dare. They'll kill me for telling you."

"No they won't. I bet they went home that night and had a good laugh about it."

Joey sighed. "Maybe."

Sam reached across the table and laid his big, warm hand over Joey's. For a moment, all the breath left Joey's body. "I'll be cool. I won't say anything."

It took Joey a moment to compose himself to nod and mumble, "Thanks."

For the rest of their limited time together, the people in the shop melted away, and they talked with Sam's hand covering Joey's.

It could never happen again.

"I had a nice time," Joey replied while brushing off an imaginary piece of lint from his shirt.

Max glanced over to Saint before continuing. "We've seen Sam stop by a few times this week. When are you guys going out again?"

"We aren't," Joey answered. It didn't surprise him that Sam's visits hadn't gone unnoticed.

"Why?" Max asked. "Was he an ass? If he did something, I wanna know."

It blew Joey's mind how protective The Gates crew could be, but he would never allow anyone to think poorly about Sam. "No, no. Sam was wonderful. He's one of the good guys."

Max looked like he wanted to carry on with the questioning, but with a shake of Saint's head, he stopped, at least regarding the handsome LAPD officer.

"Okay," Max said before leaning back in his chair. "So, how are you feeling? You've looked a bit pale recently and tired. We're concerned." Blunt and to the point, that in a nutshell was Max.

Alarms started sounding in Joey's head, but he had to keep his cool with Max. The guy was like ultra observant. "I'm feeling fine. I've always been a bit pale. My mom used to tease me by calling me Casper." *Casper? Where the hell did that come from?*

Max cocked his head to the side as if he couldn't believe what Joey said. Joey couldn't believe what he said. *Time to go.* He grabbed his backpack and said, "I'm heading out. Gotta make a few stops on my way home tonight."

Without waiting for a reply, Joey smiled at Max before turning and heading for Saint's desk. On the way, he grabbed his thin jacket off the coat tree in the corner behind the boss's desk.

"See you all tomorrow. Have a good night," Joey said on his way out the door.

With his mind racing, Joey made it out of the building and down the back stairs before anyone could stop him. Once he'd cleared the rear parking lot, he slowed his pace to match those of the other pedestrians. *Never stand out. Don't get noticed. Blend in.*

Joey would have to remind himself that while he felt safe and protected at work, he couldn't let his guard down ever. He couldn't afford to get fired, not now, when he had no safety net. The bosses were good, honest men, but Joey had been fired before when his particular condition interfered with his employment. The longer no one knew, the longer he'd have a job.

As he reached into his backpack to retrieve his water bottle, Joey realized he'd left it in the office. *Shit.* He'd have to hydrate with LA tap water when he got home to make up for the careless oversight.

Even if he didn't have a past and a family he worried people finding out about, he was panic-stricken knowing what would happen if he suffered a health crisis in front of them.

The crowds began to thin out as Joey walked farther from the main streets, and the sidewalk became darker and more menacing. The streetlights seemed to dim, and stray dogs began a chorus loud enough to wake the dead exactly like every horror movie Joey had ever seen. From one block to another, DTLA had one-bedroom condos selling for over $800k, and SROs, like the dump he lived in, that were past derelict and were queuing up for demolition.

He wasn't a coward, but he wasn't as able to defend himself as some like Sam, whose size and cop attitude was enough to scare people into minding their own. Knowing he'd be at his apartment soon, Joey picked up the pace.

As he turned the last corner before his building, he slammed straight into someone with a way more substantial body than his. He felt the jarring down to his bones.

Looking up, he realized things were a whole lot worse than bumping into some guy.

"Well, well. What do we have here?" The three men laughed as the tallest one standing in the middle pushed Joey up against the pitted brick wall.

Times like these made Joey hate his small, useless body. He might as well have a target painted on his back with flashing neon lights that read, "Mug me."

"I'm sorry, Gus. I didn't see you coming. I'll make sure never to do it again." Even as Joey said the words, he knew they'd make no difference.

Gus lived in a building down the street and had taken a personal interest in making Joey's fucked-up life even worse. He and his two goons terrorized the entire neighborhood, or at least those who couldn't fight back.

"Too late for that now," Gus growled before using the palm of his hand to slap Joey across the left side of his face. The explosion of pain was followed immediately by the iron-tinged taste of blood flooding his mouth. "Whatcha gonna give me to make up for it?"

Joey swallowed and nearly gagged on the blood before answering. "I apologized. It was an accident. I don't have anything."

"Oh, I doubt that." As if on cue, the other two went to work. One tore his backpack open and threw all the contents onto the sidewalk. The other rifled through Joey's pockets, searching for whatever they could steal. This was the reason he didn't have a cell phone, never mind that he couldn't afford one.

Joey's heart sank.

"Here we go," one of the assholes said, pulling the tip money from Joey's pocket. He hadn't stopped to hide his tips in his sock as he usually did because he'd raced out of work like the fires of hell were lapping at his feet.

"Ah, see, I knew you were hiding somethin'." Gus's cruel laugh echoed before he slapped him a second time. "That one was for lying to me. See ya around, shorty."

Joey was shoved against the wall moments before he heard the siren. Sure enough, a patrol car was headed their way from the intersection. Gus and his crew took off down the alley, and Joey knew the cops would never find them.

He struggled to bend over and pick up his few belongings while trying not to fixate on his remaining rent money, which was getting farther away from him by the second. When the cruiser finally came to a stop on the street beside him, Joey was already turning toward the front entrance to his apartment building.

"Are you okay, buddy?" the officer asked as he jumped out of his car.

"Yep, all good," Joey said while waving his throbbing hand in the air without stopping.

"Wait a minute, aren't you the guy who bartends over at The Gates? You were there at Ross's party," the officer said before he rounded the hood of the cruiser. "Yeah. Yeah, it's you. You're the one who hit Webb in the side of his head with that cork."

Ah shit. Why? Why do things keep getting worse? Haven't I paid enough for one day?

His stress level was skyrocketing exponentially, never a good situation for his health. No use in denying who he was now, doing that would be even more suspicious. "Yes, I work as a bartender at The Gates." His belly was beginning to throb. "I'm fine. They didn't get much."

"Are you sure? Your lip's bleeding, and you look white as a ghost." The officer seemed to be honestly concerned.

"Yes, I'm sure. All I want to do is have a shower and lie down." Joey tried to smile, but the look on the officer's face said he hadn't pulled it off.

"You should at least fill out a statement. We might be able to find those guys." He was persistent, if anything.

"I have no idea who they were, and we both know the odds of finding muggers in DTLA are pretty slim. I appreciate your concern, officer, but the best thing for me is to go upstairs and rest." Joey pointed up to the building beside him. "That's all I want."

The officer didn't look so sure, but Joey kept on walking up to the front doors of his building, pulled out his key and let himself in. He watched as the officer pulled away from the curb before pressing the button for the elevator.

Joey could feel his face swelling and knew he'd cut the inside of his cheek with his teeth when Gus slapped him. He'd have to make sure to refill his antibiotic prescription in case he got an infection, which was all he needed to fight right now.

The elevator dinged, and the door slid open. Seven floors later and Joey was opening the door to his small studio apartment. He made sure to throw the locks on the door and set the deadbolt. He'd had enough surprises for one day. The first thing Joey did was drop his bag, grab a glass from his one wobbly kitchen shelf, and turn on the tap to get a drink of cold water.

Though his jaw hurt, Joey gulped down the entire glass in one shot. The wrist joint on his swollen left hand was throbbing, and he prayed it would be better by work tomorrow. He'd go to work with the pain, as he'd done many times before. Hell, if he didn't work through the various aches and discomforts that were part of his usual, he'd be living on the streets or dead by now.

Stripping out of his clothing took a bit longer than usual, but he persisted and soon stood under the warm stream of water in his shower. He was so tired that he sat down on the small plastic stool he kept in the three-foot square stall for moments like these.

He soaped up and rinsed off on autopilot while his mind focused on that again he was short on his rent. Tomorrow would be his only chance to make it back in tips before his time was up. If Joey didn't come across with the money, he'd be out on his ass.

Done with his shower, he quickly dried off and didn't bother looking in his cracked bathroom mirror before taking the two steps to his dresser to put on his track pants and t-shirt. His clothes were a bit holey, but he only slept in them, so it didn't matter. He spent money on his work clothes, and even they came from thrift stores. Taking another two steps, Joey sat down on his patched futon and reached up under the frame to retrieve a small black bag.

He'd learned long ago to hide his medications and never talk about them unless he wanted someone to steal them. He took out the two clear plastic bottles with his name emblazoned on the sides along with instructions from the pharmacy. Taking medications daily had become routine, but it didn't mean he liked it. Then again, he wouldn't be too happy about the results if he didn't take them.

Trapped: his constant state of existence. Walls continued to close in on him as the years passed him by.

After filling another glass of water, he downed the medication and set the half-full glass on the floor beside his futon. There was no room for a side table, a chair, a kitchen table, or a wall unit. Joey set his small, cracked, old-fashioned television onto his dresser and ate at the counter, which was only three steps away from his futon.

Marian, The Gates's resident mom and kitchen manager, had made Joey dinner on his last break, so at least he didn't have to find food. Thankfully, all Joey had to do was crawl onto his futon and bury himself under the covers he'd received from Goodwill.

Tomorrow would be another day. Another day to fight, and another day to prevail.

At times, Joey wondered why he kept going. It would be easier to give up and surrender to his fate. Typically, at this point, he'd have already come up with a reason to carry on, but as of late, he was running out of ideas.

That one reality scared him the most.

Chapter Two

"So help me God, if one more file pops up in my inbox, the person sending it won't make it to midnight," Sam grumbled as he signed off on the last of his reports for the evening. The responding laughter from his colleagues was to be expected, since each of them felt the same way.

Three robberies, four overdoses, and a pursuit through the downtown streets thanks to a strung-out junkie had made tonight's shift feel longer than usual. Thankfully, no innocents were hurt, though an LAPD cruiser had been sacrificed to stop the runaway car after the crackhead jumped out while the vehicle was still in gear and was traveling at over thirty mph.

Welcome to another evening on shift at LAPD's Central Community Station. Sam's night could be summed up by one word: drugs. The calls he'd been on involved one illegal substance or another where the afflicted were either stealing or killing to get more, using too much and overdosing, or endangering others because of the drugs' effects. The ride went round and round, day after day, and the only way off seemed to be jail or death.

"Hey, Webb, you gotta minute?" a fellow officer asked as he neared Sam's desk.

"I'm off the clock, Ryan," Sam was quick to say. "It'll have to wait until tomorrow."

Ryan sat down anyway, making Sam growl. "Easy, man, this isn't work-related...sort of."

"Sort of?" Sam groaned, knowing whatever Ryan had to say would add another layer of bullshit to his night.

"Yeah, there was a mugging, but they got away before I could get through traffic, and the guy refused to make a statement," Ryan explained.

"And..." Sam said while he tapped his nails in a fast rhythm against his desk.

"Well, it was that guy who was working at the party for Ross. You know, at The Gates. That was the person who was mugged."

That got Sam's attention faster than anything could. "Who? Which one?"

Ryan looked at him closely. "They a friend of yours?"

"Yeah. Now, who was mugged?" Sam's patience had burnt out three hours ago.

"That short dude who hit you in the head with the champagne cork."

Sam stood. "Joey? Was he hurt?"

"Shit, man. I didn't know he was a friend of yours. I would have called you over to the scene."

Sam leaned over his desk and repeated, "Was Joey hurt?"

"Yeah, well, he looked a little roughed up, but refused care or assistance. He said he didn't know who the three men were, though I don't believe him, and that he was fine." Ryan didn't look so calm now. "Yeah, he was fine. The only blood I could see was coming from his lip. Hell, he was walking into his building when I left."

"Where?" He stuck to one-word questions, hoping to get the answers quicker.

"Over by Maria's Pizza," Ryan said. "I wrote up a report even though he didn't want to provide a statement. It should be in the system by now."

Sam sat back down and logged back into the system he'd been working on moments before.

"Sorry, man. I didn't know," Ryan said as he stood to leave.

Sam didn't bother answering. He was too busy searching through the night's reports. What should have taken seconds felt like minutes, but finally, he found it. At 20:46, a man resembling Joey was seen being held against a brick wall by a larger man as two others rifled through his backpack and pockets. When Ryan activated his siren, the three took off before he could weave through traffic and arrive on the scene.

It always amazed Sam when motorists refused to yield to first responder vehicles. Did they ever stop to think that it could be them in need of help next time? Every second counted.

Ryan noted what he could of the three other men from the distance he'd been. Odds were slim they'd be found, and whatever they'd stolen from Joey would never be recovered.

Sam's entire body tensed at the thought of anyone hurting Joey. Sure, they'd only been out once for coffee, but it had turned out to be the best coffee he'd never drank. Conversation flowed smoothly between them, and before he knew it, Sam's lunch break was over.

The couple of times Sam had popped into The Gates to say hello hadn't been enough, and he'd planned on asking Joey out to dinner. He knew they'd felt a connection, and he wanted to explore that further.

There was a building number on the report, but it was useless without an apartment number. Joey didn't have a cell phone, which was odd these days, so Sam couldn't call to check in on him. Besides, if he'd had one, it would've likely been stolen.

Sam pulled out his own cell and pulled up Ross's number. The detective knew The Gates crew a hell of a lot better than Sam did. Maybe Ross could help.

The line clicked as the call was picked up. "This had better be a goddamn emergency to be calling this late at night."

Shit. Sometimes Sam forgot that everyone didn't live on his schedule. "Sorry, Ross, but I need your help."

***

It hadn't been a restful night. *Big shock.* However, Joey managed to get out of bed. The more he moved around, the more confident he became that he could make it through his workday.

Sure, his joints throbbed, and he had bruising around the left side of his jaw, but nothing severe enough to keep him away from The Gates. A mugging would be enough of an explanation as to why he was sore when the bosses noticed his slower movements and black-and-blue marks. It would buy him a few days without anyone questioning how pale he was.

Joey had his standing appointment at Los Angeles Community Hospital with Dr. Maria Hernandez in a few days. He'd wait until then to check if his cell count was down.

His walk to work had been problem-free, as was typically the case during daylight hours. As he unlocked the back door to The Gates, Joey was beginning to feel almost passable. He took a moment to make sure the door relocked before heading to the office.

The Gates didn't open until eleven in the morning, giving Joey time to set up the bar the way he liked it before any customers arrived.

The bosses would either be in the hub or office by now, and he heard the construction workers from Max's crew working above him in the condos. Joey always enjoyed these private, uninterrupted moments walking through the elegant dining room and lounge.

The large chandeliers sparkled even when the lights were turned off, and when the sunlight from the ten-foot-tall windows hit the crystals, tiny rainbows exploded to life and seemed to float across the entire room from the curved backs of the chairs to the wrought-iron gates looming over the entrance from the foyer. The place was full of dark woods, luxurious fabrics, and warmth. He loved it here.

Feeling a bit lighter, Joey headed for the office to drop off his jacket and backpack. With any luck, Marian would have saved him something from breakfast to help him get through the day.

He turned the doorknob and walked into what only could be described as his nightmare come true, and it had him stopping in his tracks.

Sam stood with his legs apart and his arms crossed over his uniformed chest. Ross, James, Saint, Max, Finn, Miguel, and even Marian were there in a semicircle around Sam. By the looks on their faces, Joey wasn't going to like this little get-together. He considered turning around and walking right back out, but knew he wouldn't get far.

The throbbing pain in his belly was quickly moving up into his chest: the absolute worst time for that to happen.

Sam came over to him right away and gently touched the side of his face. Sam's expression was a combination of pissed off and concerned. "You okay?"

The way the gentle giant was looking at Joey's bruised jaw confirmed Sam found out about the mugging. "I'm fine, really. It was nothing."

"I'm calling bullshit. Your face and lip say what happened was more than nothing." Sam's warm thumb brushed near Joey's cut lip, making him want to melt into Sam's big, steady hand.

Before he completely lost it, Joey pulled away. "I'm perfect. I need to go get the bar ready for the day and—"

"That can wait," Saint said. "Come sit down so we can talk."

No, no, no, no, no. Talking was never a good idea. Bad things happened when bosses wanted to speak with him, like firing.

"I think I'd rather stand if you don't mind, boss." The least he could do was take it like a man, as Grandad used to say before each of Joey's punishments.

"No one is here to hurt you." Finn came over to stand beside him. "Consider this a safe place. We're all here to help."

Joey felt his mask slip for a moment but pulled it back into place quickly. But not fast enough. Finn must've seen Joey's endless well of need. He had to shut this shit down before it went any further. "I don't need any help. I was mugged, like hundreds of other residents and tourists in LA."

Ross scoffed then asked, "Do you know who the muggers are?"

Joey could feel his chest tightening as the tension in the room made him want to bolt. His blood vessels began to contract, slowing the flow of red blood cells throughout his body. He was familiar with the signs. He needed to calm down before he had a full-blown crisis because he wasn't pumping enough oxygen through his body.

"No."

"What did they take?" Max asked.

"My tips for the day." No harm in telling them that.

"How much did you lose?" Finn asked, and Joey knew the boss wanted to cover the loss.

"It's okay. I'll make it up today, no worries." There was no reason for Finn to have to pay for the mugging.

"Joey, you're getting paler," Sam commented. "Maybe I should take you over to the hospital to make sure you're fine."

Oh god no. That could never happen.

"Sam, I'm normally pale. Maybe I'm a bit tired because, obviously, I didn't sleep well last night." Yeah, that was plausible.

Pain throbbed deeper into his chest. The lack of oxygen to the tissues in his right leg felt as if there was a tourniquet strapped around his thigh. Joey wiped his sweaty palms on his pants, but that didn't help. He reached into his pocket and pulled out a tissue, forgetting that he'd put one of his pills in there to take later today if things got bad. The plain white pill fell to the floor directly in front of Sam.

Sam bent over and picked it up. The room had grown suspiciously quiet.

"Is this what last night was all about?" Sam asked while holding Joey's medication in the palm of his hand. "Drugs. Did your drug deal go bad?"

"No, no, it's not like that." Why would Sam jump to that conclusion so quickly?

"Then, what? 'Cause I sure as shit know what this is." Sam's voice deepened and became scary. Finn pulled Joey closer to him. "Opiates. Painkillers, hillbilly heroin, Roxy, any of those ring a bell? Why do you have it?" Sam's gaze had gone from warm and caring to disappointed and pissed off. Joey's sight was getting blurry, and he was becoming lightheaded.

"Why do you have painkillers in your pocket?" Max asked from across the room.

Between trying to slow his breathing and push down the pain in his chest, Joey must have taken too long to answer.

"I guess we'll have to take him down to the station and ask him there," Ross said, and that's when Joey's world began spinning. Police station, jail: they'd find out about his family. He'd be hated and fired. How would he pay for his medication or hospital bills? Fuck the rent. If they found out about his past, his life would be over. For real.

Joey felt hands wrapping around his arms before his world went dark.

Chapter Three

Sam had never felt as gutted as he did right now. Well, maybe when his sister died, but that was different. The man he was attracted to and had felt a connection with after being alone for so long was a junkie. He couldn't go through this again.

He sat in the waiting room of the ER alongside the rest of The Gates crew. Well, all except Saint and Max, who'd stayed behind to open the restaurant and bar. Sam had been beating himself up for not seeing the signs earlier: nervous with police around, secretive, weak, pale complexion, and gave ambiguous answers to common questions.

Joey had been different, or at least Sam had thought he was. How wrong could he have been?

"We can get him into treatment," Finn announced. "Addiction is a disease."

Sam couldn't help but shake his head. "I've seen dope fiends say they'd get treatment when forced, but it never lasts. Joey has to want to get help."

"Are you going to arrest him?" Miguel asked as he crossed his tattooed arms.

"No, it's useless for one pill." The chief would lose his mind, and Sam really didn't want to charge Joey.

"Then why are you still here?" James asked.

"I have no idea," Sam answered honestly.

Why had Sam stayed with his parents when they were strung out day after day? Why had he continued to take his sister to the hospital when she was found tweaking on the streets? That "take care of you" gene he had, he sure as fuck didn't inherit from his folks.

"Joey Tall's family?" a female doctor asked while looking out over the waiting room.

Finn stood up at the same time Sam did. "How is he?"

"I'm Dr. Hernandez. Joey is resting. We're going to watch over him for a few days to make sure he doesn't require another blood transfusion," the doctor explained as if this whole situation was somehow normal.

"Wait, what? Why would a junkie need a blood transfusion?" Sam asked.

"Junkie?" Dr. Hernandez scrunched up her face.

"Yeah. He was found with a prescription painkiller in his pocket," Ross said.

"While I don't agree with him only carrying a few pills at a time, I understand his worry about being robbed."

"What?" Finn asked.

"That pill you found belonged to Joey, legally. In fact, I'm the one who prescribed them to him."

The good doctor was getting nervous, and Sam began to wonder if maybe the doctor was Joey's supplier. "Why would you do that?" he asked, feeling like this might turn into a doctor dealer case, and he sure as shit didn't want Joey involved in that.

Dr. Hernandez looked at them as if they'd turned purple. "So that he could carry on with his life." She closed the screen on her tablet. "Apparently, none of you are aware of his condition, and officer, detective, you well know I cannot share his medical information with you."

"He was involved in a mugging. Could it have been to steal his drugs?" Sam asked. Somehow he had to get some concrete answers here.

"Medication. Joey is not a drug abuser, far from it." The doctor looked at them with angry disgust. "If you want any more information, come back with a warrant." She turned and walked away.

Sam didn't miss the side-glances, and all-out stares a few of the nurses were shooting his way. What the hell was going on around here?

***

Joey knew it had all been too good to last. His time at The Gates had come to a spectacular end. His colleagues had turned away from him, and so had Sam. No less than he'd experienced and expected.

He was being released today, and burning questions loomed. Did he even have an apartment to return to? It'd been two days, and Joey had already missed his rent payment. Would he even be able to get his belongings if they still existed? Joey didn't have much, but his mementos were sacred, and the little he had he'd saved for, and it would be hard to replace now that he was unemployed.

Thankfully, Dr. Hernandez had surprised him with the news that a financial donor to the hospital had set up a fund for emergencies like this that provided for Joey's medication for the next three months.

Even though he had health insurance…well, not really since he had no job and he couldn't pay the premium anymore, Joey had to pay a portion for most of his meds, and the full price the drugs not included in the health plan's formulary. Any help available was a godsend, and Joey had wanted to thank the person, but according to the doc, no one knew who they were as they preferred to stay anonymous. He could respect that and understood, considering he'd spent most of his life trying to do the same, but for entirely different reasons.

It wasn't only the medication for his pain Joey worried about. He also took antibiotics to prevent and fight bacterial infections, and another medication to improve his red blood cells' capability to hold oxygen. Then there was another drug that helped him retain calcium to prevent bone breakage. Yeah, his own blood had turned on him from the beginning of his life, much like the people in it, and both had carried on disappointing and abandoning him until the present day.

One of the hospital's social workers had been by with information on shelters in the area and soup kitchens. The more she talked about services in the city that he could make use of, the more he wanted to curl up into the fetal position and surrender to his disease.

Would he even have the energy and strength to find these places? Would people in the shelters treat him the same as Gus and his mugger pals had? Likely.

With all the things bearing down on him, the one memory Joey desperately tried and failed to keep from his mind was the look on Sam's face before Joey had passed out. The betrayal and hurt shocked and deflated him, reconfirming why he was right to never get close to people. No matter how much Joey wanted to have friends and lead a normal life, it never ended well. He spent so much effort trying to keep his body working properly, he had so little energy left over for the emotional components needed to maintain relationships.

More than once over the past few days, darker and scarier thoughts crept in, making clear how impossible it would be for someone with Joey's condition to survive on the streets. Questioning why he would even bother trying, he imagined his own painful death and thought, why not speed the inevitable along instead of suffering through the time he had left. Hell, he was one active bacterial infection away from never getting out of the hospital.

Yep, Joey knew he was in the *poor me* stage of the depression he worked hard to keep from creeping in, and he tried to push it away, but after this last incident, the depression seemed to be winning.

"So you about ready to break out of this joint?" Marian's voice startled him as she pulled the stained curtain back on Joey's small corner of the ward where he'd been placed. She set a green canvas bag at the end of his hospital bed.

Joey's mother figure for the time he'd spent at The Gates had visited him twice while he'd been hospitalized. She'd spent hours talking with him, not once asking any personal questions. He remembered being told that she had been some sort of counselor before falling on hard times and ending up on the streets.

Those same streets Joey was confident he'd soon be living on.

She'd been his only visitor.

"What are you doing here?" Joey hadn't expected to see her again. "We said our good-byes yesterday."

Marian's smile faded, and she placed her hand on Joey's arm. "Now you listen to me and do what I say. I'll help you get these clothes on, and then we're getting out of here."

Pure panic raced through him. "To where? I'm not so sure I have an apartment to return to." Or clothing, belongings, and a place to sleep, food...

"No worries, sweetheart," Marian said, cupping Joey's cheek. "I know you haven't been ready to tell me what it is you're fighting, but that doesn't mean we can't help you."

"We?" There were others involved? Who would want to help him, and why?

"Details. Now get dressed, young man," Marian ordered as she began pulling a pair of track pants, socks, underwear, and a t-shirt out of the bag she'd brought along. That small bag reminded him of a clown car. She laid out deodorant and grooming necessities, including a toothbrush, toothpaste, comb, and a razor. He was in no hurry to use the last item. His hands shook too badly.

He was humbled by the older woman's care and concern, so he didn't argue and made the decision to be as upfront with her as possible, which could be a turning point or a disaster.

"I have sickle cell disease," Joey blurted out in a rush. "Don't worry, it isn't contagious, it's genetic. I was born with it." It never ceased to surprise him how many people didn't know that and would physically pull away from him when they found out. That was the reaction that hurt the most.

Sickle cell disease had long been thought to affect only people of African descent when, in truth, anyone can be affected, though the sad truth was that the incidence of sickle cell was more prevalent in people of African descent.

The disease affected the hemoglobin in his red blood cells, which were supposed to deliver oxygen throughout a person's entire body. The disease mutated the cells to a sickle shape, and they were unable to carry enough oxygen to his system, which was when his veins and arteries began to clog up, stopping the healthy blood cells from reaching his organs and tissues. A lot of the pain he suffered was caused by parts of his body lacking oxygen.

Between fighting bacterial infections, pain, and weakness, as well as the possibility of stroke, kidney, liver, and spleen damage, his outlook was grim, and that included the likelihood he'd have an early death when he hit his forties.

This was his life, it always had been. Joey had fought from day one to be as healthy as possible. Unfortunately, now that he was on his twenty-eighth year, he was losing the will to keep fighting. His depression wasn't a surprise.

Marian's gaze never faltered. "Sweet boy. This old lady has been around the block one or two times. I'm familiar with the disease, and even if I weren't, I'd never turn my back on you."

She'd read straight through him so easily, directly to the heart of his fears. Joey nodded as he fought back the tears and slowly worked his way out of his hospital gown. His joints throbbed with pain, but at least the pain in his chest had subsided over the past two days.

The doctors were unable to give him a blood transfusion due to the iron levels in his blood being too high from previous transfusions. Joey would have to wait to see if this new medication reduced the levels enough so that he could have a transfusion in the next week or two.

Marian helped him clean up and get dressed to the point that he felt almost normal. She never tried to rush him or take over when he struggled. She seemed to know that he needed to feel healthy enough to take care of himself. She reminded him so much of his mom.

Once he'd donned his clothing, he went to the bathroom and made use of the toothpaste and other grooming stuff she'd brought. As he was walking back toward her, Joey saw her typing on her cell phone. When she'd finished, she began putting the toiletries back in the bag without saying a word.

Joey couldn't hold out any longer. "Marian, where are we going?" He tried to keep his voice calm, even as it warbled a little.

She smiled wide before answering. "Home."

"To my apartment?" Had she spoken with his landlord? Did he still have a home? Wait, how would Marian have found out how to reach the super in his building?

"No, dear, not to your apartment. Where you're going is safe, warm, and has what you need. Plus, an added bonus, I won't be far away." Was she intentionally being ambiguous in case he didn't like the answer?

"But where, Marian?"

"With us at The Gates. There's lots of space in the hub, and you'll take James's old room."

Joey wasn't sure how to feel about this new revelation. However, before he had the chance to ask more about it, Dr. Hernandez walked into the room, followed by Finn, who was pushing an empty wheelchair.

"You're all ready to go. I've been assured you'll have the support you need to continue to improve." The doctor seemed happy. Why wasn't he?

Joey looked at Finn, who wore a lopsided smile, unsure how to respond, so he simply nodded. Joey couldn't afford to get stressed out, and honestly, after everything that had transpired in the last few days, what was the worst that could happen at his new temporary digs?

"Okay then, let's grab an orderly to wheel you out." Dr. Hernandez looked over at Finn. "Hospital rules. You can't do it." She gave Finn a harsh glance, almost as if saying, "I'm watching you," before walking away. Joey couldn't help but wonder what that was all about.

"How are you feeling?" Finn asked, looking and sounding as unsure as Joey felt.

"I'm getting better every day." Joey figured he might as well get the elephant in the room dealt with. "Why are you doing this?"

"Because we care about you, and I'm an asshole." Finn huffed before he began wringing his hands. "I judged you. People have been judging me my entire life, and I did the same damn thing. I'm sorry, man. I hope, over time, we can return to the relationship we had before all this got screwed up." Finn couldn't even look Joey in the eye.

"Why are you here now? Marian has been the only one visiting me."

Finn examined the tiles on the floor as if they held the answers. "I was embarrassed by my reaction, and I didn't want to stress you more by showing up until you were feeling better. I know that was chickenshit, and I'm an asshole for not manning up."

Okay. As apologies went, that was pretty damn good. "While I should've been given the benefit of the doubt, it wasn't as though I gave you much information to go on." Finn finally looked him in the eye, and Joey could see how much this was weighing on him. "I understand, boss. I mean, sir."

"You still have a job. I've asked you to call me Finn, and you keep calling me boss. Try Finn." His smile was genuine, helping calm Joey's fears. Damn, he was thrilled he still had a job to help support himself. With the way he felt, and how long it would take to get his strength back, he couldn't imagine surviving without work and a decent place to lay his head at night.

Joey took a deep breath, his mind in a whirl, but he made a choice. He wouldn't live what remained of his life with a secret that kept him from having relationships. "I have sickle cell disease, boss."

Finn's eyes filled with tears, and he walked over to pull Joey into a gentle hug. "Thank you for trusting me with that. I swear I won't tell a soul until you're ready to do it yourself. If you choose not to, the information will go with me to my grave."

"Aww, you two getting your touchy-feely shit out of the way is damn sweet." Marian huffed. "I've got a kitchen to whip into shape before dinner tonight. Let's move it along."

Joey smiled for the first time in days. He'd honestly wondered if he would ever have a reason to do it again.

"Yes, ma'am. We can go now."

Chapter Four

Miguel stood waiting by the curb next to his car when Joey was rolled out of the hospital. Miguel looked nervous but smiled at Joey anyway. When he smiled back, the big man seemed to finally take a breath.

Given LA traffic, the drive back to The Gates seemed to take hours, and sitting in the same position in the backseat was beginning to cause his knees to throb.

"Are you okay?" Miguel asked. Joey could see the former Marine's concern in the rearview mirror. Everyone always said, "Once a Marine, always a Marine." In Miguel's case, no truer words were ever spoken. The guy was always on alert like he was on a mission.

Joey figured now was as good a time to start with the whole full disclosure thing. "My knees are beginning to hurt, but I'm used to the pain. I'll be fine." He forced a small smile to reassure the big guy the answer was honest.

Miguel nodded, the light turned green, and of course, they didn't move. The intersection was clogged with vehicles, horns were honking, people were yelling: Armageddon, or rush hour, depending on how you looked at it, had begun. By the expression on these commuters' faces, all hell was going to break loose at any moment.

Sirens blared, and flashing lights in the distance came to a stop. Soon after, they began moving again around a couple of cop cars that were buffering the accident scene. Joey could see officers up ahead, and for a second, he tensed but quickly realized the odds of seeing Officer Webb in a city as big as LA were slim at best.

Their vehicle merged into the left lane as the column of motorists were instructed to do, and inch by inch, they came upon an accident involving a school bus and a delivery truck. Thankfully, the bus looked to have been empty at the time of the crash.

The front driver's side of the bus was firmly attached to the bottom of the truck. Twisted metal lay on the road around the scene, along with pieces of glass. Joey hoped no one was seriously hurt.

That thought had barely left his mind when he found himself staring straight into a pair of dark brown eyes. Damned if he could look away. LAPD Officer Sam Webb was directing traffic around the collision, and his hand seemed to freeze in midair when his gaze latched on to Joey, who felt the weight of that stare straight down to his core. Miguel moved the car forward, and Marian took hold of Joey's hand without saying a word.

That right there is a dream too far, buddy. Get your head on straight, and stop feeling sorry for yourself. There's never gonna be a day when Sam and Joey would be anything more than brief acquaintances. Joey scolded himself for even fantasizing about a relationship with the guy. And now, since Sam thought Joey was a junkie, any explanations seemed beside the point. Yeah, once he knew the truth, Sam would apologize, but there would never be a clear path for them to travel. Not with Joey's history.

He shoved any thoughts about Sam behind a steel door in his mind where his dreams and fantasies lived, and then he locked it tight.

***

Sam paced his downtown condo from one end to the other. These walls were all that remained of his *famous* family. On a cop's salary, he'd never been able to afford to own it, but having it left to him as an inheritance meant Sam was living sweet and only had to cover the condo maintenance fees and taxes, which he could afford. Utilities would be on him no matter where he lived, and he was glad his home wasn't a shithole, or that he would've been forced to be roommates with other cops.

Even in this safe, comfortable place, eleven stories about the noise of DTLA, he couldn't sleep. Hell, he hadn't slept in days, and he was too stubborn to admit to the reason why. He had taken all the information presented to him and came to the most logical conclusion. That was what he'd been trained to do, and, more to the point, he had personal knowledge of what drug abuse looked like because of his fucked-up family. Now that he knew Joey wasn't a junkie, Sam should've felt relieved, but he couldn't throw off the mantle of guilt that blanketed him.

Seeing Joey in Miguel's vehicle had felt like a shot to Sam's stomach. He'd contacted Saint and Finn on several occasions to check on Joey's condition since Dr. Hernandez had banned him from visiting Joey in the hospital.

The Gates crew had been forthcoming. Sam knew Joey was being released today. He'd never expected to see him passing by the collision Sam was covering.

He'd frozen. Sam never froze. Not in all his years on the force, not during one of his parents' many "parties," not afterward when he would inevitably find one or both of them laid out on the floor in their own vomit. Never. Until today.

Sam still had no idea what was wrong with Joey, but the man wasn't a drug addict. That still left a whole lot of a gray area. Sam thought of everything from cancer to HIV, and different scenarios had been racing through his mind ever since.

Whatever Joey was suffering from, Sam would find a way to help. All he wanted to do was see Joey, to talk with him again the way the two of them had over coffee. To see the smile that lit up his face and laughter that could elevate anyone's mood.

So why didn't I give him the benefit of the doubt?

You know why, asshole.

His head ached as he threw himself down onto his sectional sofa and stared at the off-white popcorn ceiling. Yeah, he needed to get rid of that. He hated stereotyping. Those people who thought all gay men possessed a sense of design and style had never met him. While he wasn't medically color blind, he couldn't match more than black and white. That said, even he knew he had to hire someone to scrape the ceiling and paint it and the walls to brighten this place.

Sam had the next four days off. In that time, he'd find a way to see Joey even if he had to beg to do it. The only other time in his life that he'd begged anyone to do anything was his sister, and that was to save her life, for her to stay in treatment, but that hadn't worked out. With his batting average, Sam didn't hold out much hope that he'd be able to make things right with Joey.

***

Joey laid his sore body down on one of the softest beds he'd ever felt. He was still having a hard time believing he was here. The feeling of being safe in his own room was foreign to him. Sure, he'd felt safe working at The Gates, but now Joey was living here in the hub along with Saint, Max, and Marian. Yeah, he'd be here only temporarily, but still, the luxury of knowing he would be protected, warm, hydrated, and fed was a gift.

Initially, the room had been Finn's until he'd moved in with his boyfriend, Miguel. Then James, Finn's brother, had stayed in it before hooking up with Detective Ross. Now it was Joey's, and it had been a long time since he'd felt this kind of comfort. Though the "finding love" streak the people who'd stayed in this room had enjoyed had come to an end.

The room had been recently re-drywalled and painted, and the bed, dresser, and night tables looked new. Joey even had a forty-eight-inch smart TV. He'd never seen a picture so clear that he had thought he could actually reach out and touch the people in it.

A little over twenty-four hours had passed since he'd arrived back at The Gates, and so far, he had mainly remained in his room. His strength was returning slowly, and he figured it'd still take a few more days before he was up to wandering around. This crisis hadn't been any worse than similar health events, but he noticed the older he got, the longer it took for him to recover from any type of health-related problem. Now, a crisis set him back weeks instead of days.

Marian had brought him food, and Finn and Saint visited regularly. The next day he hoped to make it out to the central part of the hub to sit on the couch and feel normal. Talk with the guys and explore his new world as a resident of The Gates. Maybe, in a couple days, he might feel well enough to return to bartending, at least part-time. Joey refused to be a freeloader. He'd earn his keep.

Though there was little he had of any value, Joey was waiting to hear back from his former landlord to arrange a pickup of his belongings. It wasn't looking promising. Among the few things that mattered were two items of his mother's, and Joey would do anything to get those back.

A soft knock sounded, bringing Joey back out from his thoughts. "Come in."

His door opened, and Finn popped his head in. "Up for a visit?"

"Sure. Between sleeping and watching home improvement shows, I'm going a little stir-crazy. I could use the company." Joey waved Finn into the room.

Joey pushed himself up on the bed and leaned against the headboard so that Finn could sit beside him.

"Nothing else on?" Finn asked as he picked up the remote control.

"I kinda like watching them," he admitted, and Finn set the remote down. "Mostly, I love to see the before and after shots, where they take something old and broken, and make it beautiful again. It's satisfying."

Finn nodded his head in what Joey thought was understanding, and in a way, he imagined Finn did. Considering he'd rebuilt his own world a couple of times over the years, from cult survivor to living on the streets, to now managing The Gates and feeding the homeless on his days off, Finn had persevered. Joey respected that and hoped to emulate that kind of transformation.

They sat in companionable silence, watching an old arts and crafts bungalow come back to life with a new paint scheme. Joey's mom used to read design magazines and left them lying around the house for him so he could look at the pictures. His granddad's home resembled the old Craftsman house, or at least what he remembered of it.

"Have you heard back from your old landlord yet?" Finn asked.

Joey had shared his concern about his belongings when he'd arrived at The Gates from the hospital. He'd called his former landlord immediately and left a message but hadn't received a call back.

"No, not yet." He didn't hide his disappointment and worry.

"We'll figure something out. I promise."

"Thanks, but you've already done so much. The picture of my mom and her necklace are probably already gone by now. I think it might be a lost cause." Joey hated to give up, but he certainly wasn't going to drag his boss into it. Finn nodded as if he'd accepted what he had said, but Joey wasn't so sure that he did.

"There's, um… something I need to ask you," Finn said during a commercial break.

"Oh no," he accidentally groaned aloud.

What had he done? Were they changing their minds about having him stay in the hub? Was he too much trouble? Did they find out about Joey's family ties to the mob and his grandfather Bishop Venzezo's role as the head of the rattlesnake? Possible scenarios raced through Joey's mind. Even though he hadn't seen or spoken to his grandfather in over nineteen years, he still worried.

Finn was quick to say, "No, no, it's nothing bad. You don't have to worry."

Joey was still a little on guard. "Okay, what do you need?"

"Sam wants to come to visit you."

"Umm." Joey wasn't sure he'd heard him right. "I'm sorry, what?"

"I wouldn't even have brought it up if the guy hadn't been checking in daily on your recovery, and is now pretty much begging to see you." Finn shrugged. "I know he made an asshole move, we all did, but after James told me about Sam's past...."

"His past?" If anyone understood about having a past that colored your view on life, it was Joey.

"It's not my story to tell. Detective Ross has known Sam for years, and all I'm saying is maybe there was more to his reaction then any of us knew at the time. Don't get me wrong. I'm not trying to convince you that he wasn't wrong in jumping the gun. But if you're willing to hear him out, he wants to see you."

Where to start with this turn of events? Joey wanted to see Sam, and he didn't. Talk about conflicted. He worried what Officer Webb was going to say, and if Sam had a different take than the man he was when he wore his badge. If Joey had to guess, if they weren't one and the same, he'd be surprised.

"Is he coming here as Officer Webb or as Sam?"

"Sam. Simply Sam," Finn assured. "I understand you wanting to know the difference, make the distinction. I've been taken away in cuffs a few times in my life. Mainly for vagrancy."

Joey wanted nothing to do with visiting a police station for any reason. However, the real question was, should he say no, keep Sam out of his life? In the end, it would make a lot of things a hell of a lot easier for both of them. Then again, when had he ever done things the easy way?

"When would he be coming over?"

"Whenever you say it's okay."

After a few moments, they lapsed into silence, their attention seemingly on the television show. Clearly, Finn wasn't going to press him to make a decision, and for that, Joey was thankful. He'd given in to his need to get closer to Sam when he'd accepted his offer of coffee, which had turned out to be amazing, and a small part of him still believed in the dream of a different life.

But things had changed. Reality had sucker-punched him with the truth. He was sick, and at best, the doctors agreed the disease guaranteed he'd make it only to his mid-forties. At twenty-eight, time was ticking by faster than ever since the finish line was that much closer. Even if he and Sam could come to mean something to each other, wouldn't that make Joey a cruel bastard?

While wallowing in self-pity held a certain appeal, Joey had accepted his fate long ago. He wasn't going to be dragging anyone else down with him.

With that in mind, he said, "Sam has to understand we could never be more than friends. Before he comes here, he has to know that."

Finn looked at him closely, and for once, Joey didn't bother to hide what he was feeling or even try to smile it away.

"I'll make sure he understands that."

"Good." Even though the easier path was to tell Sam not to come, Joey gave in to wanting some slim slice of happy. "Sam can come to visit with me tomorrow morning."

"I'll let him know."

With that made clear, they turned their attention back to the show. Sure enough, by the end, the little bungalow looked better than new. The homeowners cried on cue after the big reveal, and Joey wished them happiness in their new home, as he always did.

As his mom used to say, never resent someone who appears to have more than you financially, physically, or emotionally. We all have struggles to overcome. Some simply carry a heavier load.

Chapter Five

Sam felt like he was staring down a firing squad. Finn, Miguel, Saint, and Max stood at the entrance to the hub, their expressions the solemn masks of men guarding a fallen colleague.

"You know how Joey wants it: friends. Don't go getting all romantic or anything because we all here know how you feel about him," Max warned. "Even after what happened that day."

"Message received. If friendship is all I can have, I'll take it."

"He'll have to forgive you first," Finn reminded. His eyebrow raised, a not-subtle indication he was judging Sam's worth.

"I realize that." That was the first and most important part of his plan.

Before anyone else could say another word, Marian walked in carrying a tray with plates full of food on it. "Since you're here, you can make yourself useful and take this to Joey. He needs to eat *all* his breakfast, make sure of it." Marian thrust the tray into his hands and turned to look at the assembled posse. "What are you all standing around for, moral support? We have a business to run here, a lounge to open, along with the dining room. Max, don't you have a crew upstairs working on the condos that might require your attention? Move it."

Sam hid his smile at the disgruntled looks of the other men, but no one argued. After a chorus of "yes ma'am's," the group dispersed.

"Go, he needs to eat," Marian said as she shoved Sam toward the hallway that led to Joey's room.

"Um, thank you, Marian."

"Don't thank me yet," she warned. "I'm still watching you. Joey has a soft spot when it comes to you, and that's the only reason you're here."

"Understood, ma'am."

Marian had helped him escape from further interrogation, but she wasn't letting him off the hook. He deserved that and respected her all the more for saying it to his face.

Sam took a deep breath and started down the hallway. *Had it always been this long?* It seemed to take minutes to cross the twenty-five feet. His heart was pounding to the rhythm of a death march in his chest, but he wasn't turning back. This meant too much to him.

Joey had to forgive him. Even if he had to spend the rest of his life making up for his stupidity, Sam would earn Joey's trust back. This was more than an apology. Aside from making sure Joey understood Sam knew he'd been a judgmental ass, this was a bit of Sam taking back a part of his soul. Yeah, he was jaded with good reason, but if he didn't make room for explanations and forgiveness, he would wind up alone and bitter.

He balanced the food tray in one hand and knocked on the door. When he heard Joey's voice welcoming him in, Sam reached for calm and turned the doorknob.

The first thing he noticed was all the flowers and then Joey sitting fully dressed on a plush chair beside a small table. Should he have brought flowers?

At least, Joey wasn't as pale as he'd been days ago. That had to be a good sign, right?

"Finn's insane," Joey said matter-of-factly.

Sam was caught off guard. "What?"

"The flowers are his fault. He has to be stopped," Joey explained while waving his hands at the surrounding foliage.

Sam scanned the room and saw at least six large bouquets. "It's…um, impressive."

"It's crazy. I'm surprised I haven't been swarmed by bees when I open the window for some fresh air." Joey couldn't hide his smile, making Sam's anxiety ratchet down a few notches.

Sam couldn't help but smile at Joey. The man was adorable. Though he doubted Joey would appreciate the characterization. The handsome man may be small in stature, but he had an internal strength not many could match.

"I brought you breakfast," he said as he placed the tray on the table and set his backpack down on the floor. "Marian made me promise, you have to eat it all."

They looked down at the heaping plate of breakfast goodness. Three sunny-side-up eggs, four pieces of toast, three pieces of bacon, two sausages, hash browns, and a cup of cubed fresh fruit. How much did she think Joey could eat?

"Maybe you can help me eat it, but we'll keep that between us," Joey said. "I'd rather stay on Marian's good side."

Sam could understand feeling that way, because so did he. The woman was fierce.

"Okay, but you eat as much as you can before I take anything." He wanted Joey to capitalize on all the nutrients before Sam ever took a bite.

"Deal," Joey agreed happily, leaving Sam feeling they'd made an agreement to more than breakfast. He didn't care. As long as Joey kept smiling, he'd do anything to keep that look on his face.

***

Joey watched as Sam sat down in the chair on the other side of the table. He took the plates and bowl off the tray, along with the orange juice, and set them between them. Reaching back, Joey opened the side table's top drawer and retrieved the bottle containing one of his medications. Joey had to take it with food or it upset his stomach, and he didn't need to make himself any sicker.

Here would be the test, of sorts. He turned back around to face Sam, popped the bottle open, and fished out a single pill. Instead of the looks of disappointment and judgment he'd expected, Joey saw guilt and sadness.

"I have to take it with food, so I don't become nauseous," he explained. Hoping to ease whatever Sam was feeling.

"Joey, I'm sorry," Sam said. "I'm sorry for accusing you and not allowing you the time to explain. I was wrong, so wrong that I feel sick. I don't care what you have. Wait, I do care, but you don't have to tell me. I'll never pressure you into revealing it. I wanted you to know my behavior was unacceptable and cruel, but I'm hoping you can give me a chance to fix our friendship."

Joey could feel the anxiety pouring off Sam. He looked tired, and the dark circles under his expressive eyes broadcast he wasn't sleeping well.

For a moment, Joey fantasized that he'd been the cause of Sam's sleepless nights, but he knew better than to indulge in such childish thoughts; they weren't allowed space in his brain any longer.

Easy enough to let the guy off the hook. Joey said, "Well, it wasn't as if I gave you a whole lot of information to go on. I imagine you see the results of illegal drug activity on the streets most days on the job."

"I do, but it gave me no right to say the things I did to you. You've never seemed drugged out, only tired. You work hard, and always have a smile or a kind word for everybody. How could I have thought so poorly of you, when all you've been is…perfect?"

"I'm so far away from perfect you won't even find me on the same map," Joey teased.

Sam smiled. "Eat before your food gets cold. We can talk more after you're full, if you want." Sam's knee bounced up and down in a steady rhythm, belying his calm and encouraging words.

"Sure, sounds great." Joey picked up his fork and dug into the mound of hash browns. Joey loved potatoes no matter how they were prepared. Which was good because they were usually cheap to buy and lasted a while. He'd had potatoes for dinner many times.

They sat in companionable silence while Joey ate, the only sound coming from one of his home shows, which was playing on the TV in the background. He watched Sam take a game console and two controllers from his backpack along with a couple games.

"What's that for?" Joey asked, and the moment the question left his lips, he groaned. Of course, it was designed to play video games. "I meant, what are you planning to do with it."

"The console is for you. It will entertain you while you're healing," Sam said with a grin. "Nothing wrong with a bit of a distraction."

Joey nodded, but his brain was stuck on *healing*. He wished it were so easy. Rest, recoup, and come out stronger and healthy. No, not in the plans set out for him since birth. He'd always have this disease, and it was only going to get worse.

Sam looked at him closely. "What's wrong?"

Honesty was his new mantra concerning his health, at least. "Sam, I'll never heal from what I have." There you go, let the chips fall where they may.

Sam took a moment before answering. "I understand. Is there anything I can do to help you?"

"You're not going to ask me what it is I have? Or if I'm contagious?" That's a first. Well, maybe not, considering The Gates crew's reactions to his illness. This whole episode was out of the ordinary and left Joey in unfamiliar territory. He was more used to rejection than anything else.

"No, I don't need to know, and as far as being contagious, you're far too kind to hurt anyone else. So, I'm betting you're not."

"I'm not," Joey confirmed. Sam smiled as if he didn't have a care in the world. "Why are you so happy?"

"Because I'm here with you."

Joey wasn't sure how to respond to that, so he went back to his meal. Sam walked over to the television and began hooking up wires to the game console. Joey was curious about what type of games the big LAPD officer preferred to play: war games and westerns, or fantasy and mythical creatures. He slid the small pile of games sitting on the table closer to check them out. One after the other, they were all racing games, every last one.

"I don't like to play video games with guns," Sam explained. "I live with a gun strapped to my body for work. Any break I can get from that is welcome."

That made sense. Joey wouldn't want to carry a gun around all day and then go home and relax with a violent game. He'd never be able to relax.

"I warn you, I haven't played this type of video game in a long time. I believe the last time I was about ten years old. I'll need a crash course."

"Done. No worries," Sam assured before taking over the plate of food Joey had pushed in front of him. "I'll get you up to speed in no time. Get it, speed-racing." He laughed at his own joke, and Joey shook his head. Sam was a goofball.

Joey's emotions had been all over the place in recent days, but for now, he was happy, and he would take that feeling for as long as it was offered.

Once Sam finished their shared plate of food, he got up and carried his chair over to in front of the television before coming back for Joey's.

"Can I lift your chair for you?" he asked, without being condescending.

Joey was shocked again. Sam didn't assume Joey couldn't do it, he asked if he could help. Joey didn't like it when people treated him as if he were made of glass because of his disease. Even Marian, who doted on all of them, did so in a gruff, no-nonsense kind of way. Joey appreciated that, and he was happy Sam seemed to be acting the same way as The Gates crew. Though he couldn't predict what would happen from one day to the next, for the most part, Joey was bedbound. He needed to feel as if he was being treated like anyone else, even if he was still too weak to lift the damn chair.

"Yes, please," Joey answered as he stood. "My mom and I used to play all kinds of games. She loved the one with those two Italian brothers, and we'd stay up late on the weekends playing it over again. She died when I was young. Do you still have your parents?"

Sam paled and looked away before saying, "Let's sit down, and I'll tell you all about them."

Joey did what he'd been asked, now unsure if he shouldn't have said anything. Lots of people didn't like to talk about their family. He didn't even know who his bio father was.

Sam handed him one of the controllers before saying a word. Maybe he was trying to decide on how much to say. "It's okay, Sam. You don't have to tell me anything. It's cool."

Sam turned in his chair to face Joey straight on. "I want you to know more about me, and my childhood is the place to start. To answer your initial question, no, my parents and sister are deceased."

"I'm sorry. I didn't mean to pry."

"Of course, you didn't. How could you have known?" Sam assured him. "I was born at Cedars-Sinai to relatively famous parents. Nannies raised my sister and me because our parents were either away on set, or partying with their friends. I didn't know anything different from that life. The first time I realized that my parents weren't the same as my friends' parents was when I was invited to a sleepover party. I think I was around eight at the time.

"The boy's parents were both there waiting for me to be dropped off by our driver. Then they walked us into the kitchen, where they were cooking up treats and dinner while laughing and making a fuss over all the kids. It all felt so different than what I was used to.

Cooks in the kitchen, nannies taking care of my sister and me... I wanted what my friend had, but my folks weren't like that."

Joey watched the pain and longing as it traveled across Sam's handsome face. Joey's mom may have died young, but all those moments when they were together were filled with precious memories. Sam had been denied that comforting love from a parent.

"The next few years were a whirl of award shows, movies, and parties. They did rich well. On my fourteenth birthday, I waited for hours for them to come out of their master bedroom. Finally, when the sun began to set, I got fed up and stormed into their room, demanding to know how they could have forgotten my birthday. There were five of them in that huge bed of theirs. Ashtrays, empty bottles, and pills surrounded them in their island of overindulgence and debauchery. They didn't even wake up."

Joey took hold of Sam's hand, trying to offer comfort while thinking how hard it must've been for a young Sam to see such a thing.

"Looking back, I realized that year the partying had picked up. I lost count of how many times I'd found them stoned out of their minds. My younger sister, Jessica, wanted us to move in with our grandmother, but they refused to let us go. It would have been a scandal, and they were all about appearances. They didn't give a shit about their kids. But their reputations had to remain perfect in the public eye."

The whole pill thing was starting to make sense now. Sam's reaction was exacerbated by what he'd lived through as a child. It didn't mean that he was blameless in making assumptions about Joey, but it sure as hell explained how Sam *went there*. Maybe this was what Finn had been talking about yesterday. Joey squeezed Sam's hand even tighter.

"Over the next few years, my sister fell into a deep depression and began stealing our parents' drugs to escape. They'd never even noticed. Neither had I until I came home early from college for Christmas break. No one was expecting me, and as usual, my parents weren't even home. So I went to Jessica's room to surprise her. I remember being so excited to see her. I'd been away for months."

Joey could feel a slight tremble work its way down Sam's arm. Whatever he must have found had shaped the man he was today.

"She was still a senior in high school, so when I heard voices coming from her room, I assumed it was a school friend over because it was barely after four in the afternoon. As it turns out, that was another bedroom door I shouldn't have opened." Sam shook his head as if the motion could rearrange the memories. "Jessica was in bed with a man over twice her age. I recognized him from one of my parents' parties. That, along with the pills and alcohol, set me off. I grabbed the guy and threw him and his clothes out of my sister's room. It didn't take long for the asshole to find the front door. When I came back, I found Jess laughing hysterically in between long pulls on a fifth of whiskey.

"She attacked me when I tried to pry it out of her hands. Eventually, I was able to calm her down and call for an ambulance. My sister was out of her mind on whatever she'd taken. I knew I had to get her help."

"I understand." Intellectually, he could process what he was hearing, but he couldn't imagine coming home to find his sister that way. For the most part, Joey wasn't into confrontation, but had it been him, he probably would've beaten that guy to a pulp.

"The paramedics showed up and took her over to the hospital. Jess had to be restrained to the bed with harnesses on her ankles, waist, and wrists to prevent her from hurting herself and someone else. I stayed with her all night, sitting in a chair beside her bed. I'd known why she'd done what she did. I understood it. The difference between us was she leaned into what they did and who they were. I couldn't get far enough away from it fast enough."

Sam sighed. Clearly, talking about this was wearing on him. "The next morning, our parents finally showed up. Their dark sunglasses didn't fool me. They were stoned. But considering they'd had years of working in that condition, they could pass as lucid to anyone else. They appeared to be A-list celebrities walking the halls behaving as if they were gracing us with their presence with their dark sunglasses, designer clothing, and demeanor."

"I'm sure they were thankful you saved your sister's life," Joey said before realizing that Sam had mentioned at the beginning that Jessica was dead. Before he could apologize, Sam carried on with his heartbreaking past.

"I thought so, but I soon found out they were pissed off. Reporters had gotten wind of the whole episode, and they were splashing pictures of Jess being loaded into an ambulance in all the rag papers and gossip TV shows. My parents were furious with me. When my father made me leave my sister's hospital room, she was still unconscious. I didn't get the chance to talk to her. After they moved me into an empty room, they shut the door and lost their shit. I was ordered back to my college and was warned to stay there. I started to fight with them, and they swore they'd get Jess into treatment. That this had been a one-time event, but they would fix it." He scowled. "I should have known whatever they did was to maintain their image. I had two more years left of college, and after I graduated, I went to the police academy. To say my parents were unimpressed with my career choice would be an understatement."

Yeah, Joey could picture Sam's parents as they realized their son was going to be putting people like them in jail for a living. It reminded Joey of when his granddad found out that his only grandson wasn't perfect and had sickle cell disease. A chronically sick kid couldn't take over the family business, especially when that business was all kinds of violent and illegal.

"No one showed up to my graduation ceremony. When I was hired on by the LAPD, I got my own apartment and begged Jess to move in with me. She had to get away from our parents. Jess would never get clean staying with them. Not surprised, she refused. She even went as far as trying to convince me that she was fine. I didn't buy it, but I had no control over the situation. Jess was over eighteen, and could do as she pleased."

Sam sat in silence for several minutes, and Joey didn't rush him. He had to get the story out in his own way and in his own time.

He clasped his hands between his thighs and continued. "It didn't take long for Jess to show up on the streets of DTLA strung out, but it was already too late. She didn't even recognize me when I picked her up staggering down Third Street. I was still on duty and took her to the hospital. The doctors and nurses at the ER knew me and promised they'd look after her. I had to return to my shift, but by the time I made it back to the hospital, Jess had taken off. I searched for her for days and was even so desperate that I went as far as calling my parents. Of course, they didn't answer. A week later, Jess was found dead in a crack house on the south end of the city."

"I don't know what to say. 'Sorry for your loss' seems trite and shallow," Joey said while leaning closer to the big guy.

"It's okay. It was over ten years ago. I've made my peace with it. A couple years after Jess's death, I was in line at the supermarket and saw on the front page of a paper that my parents had overdosed. I had them buried over in Forest Lawn, alongside Jess."

Joey reached over and wrapped his arms as far as he could around Sam, hugging him with the little strength he had. Sam hugged Joey back.

Yeah, Mom had been right. You never truly knew the weight someone else was carrying.

Chapter Six

After true confessions and the hug session, Joey asked about the video games, and Sam was thankful. He hadn't wanted to unload like that, but he figured if Joey knew his background, it would help explain his rush to judgment. Sam taught Joey the rules of one of the games, and they began to have fun playing his favorite racing game, Chill to Thrill.

The premise of the game was one minute your avatar is chilling, parked on the street, and then something massive happens, making you have to race through the city. Sam liked that the player never knew what catastrophe would hit and when. It was completely random. Joey had loved playing, and by the end, he wasn't slamming into walls, parked cars, or other vehicles as much.

Joey was nearly asleep when Sam left the room. Quietly, he shut the door and headed for the kitchen to return the tray and plates. The hub was empty, and The Gates had begun lunch service. Sam dodged a few waiters carrying large trays heaping with food as he came out into the central area of activity. It smelt so good in there that it made his stomach growl. Sam had to admit, the level of dining in this part of the downtown area had undoubtedly picked up since Saint had opened his restaurant and lounge.

Sam went through one of the kitchen's swinging doors and stood in the middle of organized madness. The kitchen staff worked like a well-oiled machine. Separate areas were designated for a specific purpose. Sam saw prep areas, cooktops, ovens, and a pastry section, but what he knew about commercial kitchens and cooking was limited, so he guessed at what he took in.

One thing that couldn't be missed was at the front dead center of all the mayhem stood Marian, confident and watchful. She inspected each plate before it went out to the tables.

Sam didn't want to get in the way, so he set the tray down near the dishwashers and turned to leave when he heard an argument coming from farther in the back. He followed the noise, wanting to make sure that someone didn't need assistance, and found Finn, Saint, and Max standing in a circle in the stockroom. Arms and voices were raised as they continued to argue.

"You are not going there alone, and that's final," Saint ordered. "Anything could happen to you."

"Have you forgotten that I'm my own person and capable of making my own choices?" Finn asked while waving his hands in the air. "Look, you're my friend and boss, but you're not my father."

"True. But Miguel's out of town on a mission, and we promised to watch over you," Max said while placing himself between Finn and Saint.

"Am I twelve?"

"You're acting like you are when you think you can go over to Joey's old apartment and deliver that alone. We can't leave The Gates at the moment to come along. It'll have to wait." Saint's face was flushed. They must have been arguing for a while now.

"But we have to move quickly before he gets rid of Joey's belongings, especially those mementos from his mom." Finn's tone had changed from anger to resignation, signaling he already knew he wasn't going anywhere.

"I can go with him," Sam said, alerting the three men to his presence.

He'd expected to see anger directed at him for interrupting their discussion, or for even being in the stockroom. It wasn't as if Sam worked here. Instead, he recognized relief when he saw it.

"Are you available now?" Saint asked.

"Yeah. I'll drive."

Finn came over to stand beside Sam and said, "Thank you. I don't want Joey to lose what few precious things he has left in his life."

"I completely understand. Neither do I," Sam agreed. "What's the plan?" If there was a chance of getting Joey's property back, he was all in.

"Finn not getting punched out by that asshole Frank Greeve, whose lording over the building as if it were his own kingdom or something, is a good place to start," Max said.

"Small dog syndrome," Finn said. When they all turned to look at him, he continued, "You know, the small dog that acts like a big dog. I don't know what to call it in humans, maybe elevated ego or something."

"Finn will be safe with me," Sam stated. He lifted his chin at what was in Finn's hand. "What's in the envelope?"

"We had our lawyer write up a formal request for entrance into Joey's old apartment to pick up a few things. If Greeve doesn't allow it, we'll have to take him to court. On the other hand, if Joey's belongings are already gone, Greeve better hope he has a good lawyer," Saint threatened.

"With the extenuating circumstances brought on by Joey's illness, we should have been given time to remove his stuff. So far, he's refused," Max explained.

"So, you want to go to serve him the papers, get whatever is left of Joey's belongings, and you need a bodyguard and a witness to do that." Sam wanted to make his responsibilities clear.

"Exactly." Finn gave hi-five with a broad smile on his face.

"Got it. Let's go."

Sam pulled up to the front of Joey's former apartment building, if you could call it that. One of the last SROs in DTLA, especially in this neighborhood where, street by street, new buildings and renovations like The Gates were under way, this piece-of-shit eyesore stood out for all the wrong reasons. A flashy BMW 8 Series was parked ahead of him, a flashing neon sign of a likely drug dealer surrounded by the other POS vehicles lining the street. A man appeared to be waiting in the driver's seat.

Since the guy and the car weren't breaking any laws, Sam couldn't approach, but his gut told him differently. What he'd give for his police vehicle and its mobile data terminal right now. He'd be sure to jot down the license plate number as a precaution.

"You ready to do this, Finn?" Sam asked the twitchy dude beside him.

"Oh yeah. I want a piece of that scumbag," Finn said without a shred of fear.

"We're not here to get into a fistfight." Sam wanted to make that clear.

"I won't start it, but if he becomes aggressive, I will defend myself."

"I'm positive you would. However, that's the reason I'm here, remember that. Miguel will kill me, after torturing me, if there's even a single scratch on you. Let's go."

Finn responded with a cheeky smile. *Brat.* This might get interesting. Sam would have to stay on guard because Miguel was no joke when it came to his protectiveness over Finn.

Sam grabbed his notepad and a card out of the glove box, then they got out of his 2011 Volkswagen Jetta. It was reliable and still in pretty good shape. *If it ain't broke, don't fix it.* Although having the cars parked close together, it wasn't hard to see the dichotomy between the two worlds. But Sam knew the price of that world and was happy to remain where he'd chosen to be.

He reached for the front door of the building at the same moment a large, dark-haired man wearing a three-piece suit and sporting a scar down the left side of his face pushed the door open. He barely missed Sam's outstretched hand.

"Get out of my way," the stranger grumbled before barreling between them on his way to the back door of the BMW. A blacked-out SUV came around the corner and stopped in the middle of the street to let the asshole's car out into traffic, then followed the BMW. Interesting.

"Well, shall we?" Finn asked, now holding the door open for Sam. "Don't worry about that jerk, there's plenty more where he came from." Finn had lived on the streets for a good part of his life and, as such, had front row seats to the underbelly of society.

"And where would that be?" Sam asked.

"You know, the sprawling estates outside of the city where all the billionaires live. It doesn't matter if your money is dirty or not, as long as you have enough of it."

"Hmm, yeah, you have a point."

Once they were inside, it wasn't difficult to find Mr. Greeve's apartment. No matter where Sam looked, there were obnoxious signs the size of a car window proclaiming the space as the super's office. The man certainly wanted the tenants to know who was in charge around here.

Finn looked up at Sam for a brief moment before knocking on the door, making Sam wonder how much of his fear Finn was hiding behind his calm demeanor. Sam wouldn't allow anyone to touch him.

"What do you want?" A man who looked to be in his early fifties growled as he yanked open his apartment door.

The smell hit Sam first, like a mix of vomit and shit. Greeve wore a stained t-shirt that Sam assumed had once been white, and a pair of holey silk boxers. His stomach hung a good eight inches over his waistband. The comb-over didn't hide the balding head, and the cigarette in his hand was the source of the gust of smoke the jerk was now blowing into their faces.

Finn coughed but quickly recovered and said, "Mr. Greeve, this is for you." Then pushed the envelope into the super's dirty hands. The man had no idea what personal hygiene was, or if he did, he certainly didn't care.

The front door of the building opened again, allowing two women who were carrying a few bags of groceries into the hallway. When they crossed in front of Greeve's door, they made sure to stay against the wall farthest away from him.

The dirty sleazeball grabbed the front of his boxers, causing parts of his testicles to fall out of one of the many holes. Sam was definitely going to take an interest in Greeve from this point on after they got what they came for. Sam repositioned himself in a way that if the asshole made a move toward the women, Sam would be able to stop him.

"I'll be seeing you whores later." Greeve laughed as the two quickly unlocked their apartment door, which was located down the hall, before rushing in. Sam heard six locks closing as they bolted the door behind them.

"You have that effect on all the women who live here, Mr. Greeve?" Sam asked as he pulled out his notepad and began taking notes, or at least making it look that way.

"Women are whores, only good for one thing, you know."

"No, I'm sure I don't," Sam replied.

"What are you taking notes for?" Greeve asked, scrunching his face up as if he'd finally smelled the odor wafting from his body.

Sam played it up. He was the son of actors, after all. "Oh, where are my manners," he said before pulling his LAPD business card out from his pocket and handing it over to the soon-to-be-former super if Sam had anything to do with it. He wasn't leaving a predator in this position to continue his harassment. "I'm taking notes as a witness.

Wouldn't want to forget anything." Then he pulled out his cell phone and took a picture of Greeve.

"Witness for what? Why did you take my picture?" Greeve asked before looking down at the business card in his hand. His eyelids opened wide when the realization hit him. "A cop? What's this all about? Don't you need a warrant or somin'?"

"No, I'm not here in an official capacity, and I don't intend to enter your apartment." Lord knows what he'd find in there, never mind what disease he would catch. "I'm filling in as a witness in case this ends up in court, and the picture is to jog your memory in case you have a bout of amnesia."

Finn was watching the confrontation closely. Sam wanted to smile. This asshole was more bark than bite. He thought about what Finn said regarding small dog syndrome. This guy was most definitely a Chihuahua.

"You might want to open that letter before we carry on with any further discussions," Finn advised in a cold, professional tone. Good, no emotions at all. Never show weakness.

Greeve shoved Sam's card into his waistband before tearing into the letter. He took a few minutes to read it as his face turned a deeper shade of red by the second. Sam placed his hand in front of Finn and pushed him back out of the way in case lover boy went berserk.

"Fuck. What is it about this measly kid?" Greeve huffed out as he ground the end of his cigarette under his foot.

Sam found that question odd. "What do you mean?"

Then he saw it, fear, racing across his face. "Nothin'. Here take his shit and go. I never want to see him back here again," Greeve said while shoving a key into Sam's hand.

"Don't worry, he's never coming back here," Finn answered.

Sam wasn't buying the "nothin'" Greeve was trying to sell, but he had no evidence to the contrary. He took the key before Greeve slammed the door in their faces.

"Righteous. We can go get Joey's stuff," Finn cheered, took the key from Sam's hand, and headed for the elevator.

Sam followed. His instincts told him more was going on with this landlord than merely being a pervert, a slob, and living out his fantasy of being the king of the building. Sam would definitely have to take a closer look into this because if it involved Joey, Sam wanted a heads-up so he could protect him.

Chapter Seven

Bishop Venzezo sat behind his handcrafted teak desk, contemplating his next move. He wrapped his lips around his cognac-aged cigar while holding a glass of seventeen-year-old scotch in his left hand. He exhaled a cloud of smoke and watched as the sweet tendrils branched out before him.

Money and power blanketed him, affording him any luxury he desired. A lot of good his wealth did him now. The one thing he desperately needed was missing, and until he turned up, they had to wait.

Patience wasn't one of his best qualities, and his organization knew this and explained why so many of the smaller kingpins had their guys out searching for Bishop's prize. No one wanted to feel his wrath. It was the quickest way to earn a trip out into the Pacific for a midnight swim.

The knock on his study door was unwelcome, and he growled his reply. "Knock again, and I'll take your hand."

The voice of his closest lieutenant, Razor, echoed through the closed door. "I don't want to bother you, sir, but the gentleman you spoke with today is here and saying he has some information you'll want to hear."

"Greeve?"

"Yes, sir."

"This better be important. Bring him in." Bishop downed the last of his scotch and snuffed out his cigar. He'd have time to enjoy the rest of it later.

The double doors opened wide before that sniveling bastard was dragged in. Two of Bishop's men had him by the arms while two stood beside the doors. "I told you to disappear, Greeve, and now you're here in my home. Do I have to sew your mouth shut and cut off your legs to make that happen?"

His men laughed. They'd enjoy a little recreation. He hadn't had a guest down in his cellars for some time. Maybe this was what he needed to work off some of his stress.

"No, sir. I wouldn't have come here, Bishop, if I didn't have information on that man you came looking for." Greeve was down on his knees, head bowed, shaking like a man at the gallows. Precisely the way Bishop liked it.

Never call me by my name," he bellowed. "I doubt you have anything more than what my men have found combing the city."

"We'll get rid of him, boss," Razor said while reaching for Greeve, who was trying to scurry away on all fours.

"No, it's true. I have something that'll help you find him," Greeve begged while digging his nails into an expensive Persian area rug to stop from being dragged from the room. "People came to get his stuff out of his apartment."

That got Bishop's attention. "Let him go." Instantly, the foul-smelling man was dropped onto the ground. Power was his alone, and others acted accordingly. "Who were they?"

Greeve fished a card out from under his sizable stomach. Bishop wasn't touching that. He'd likely come away with hepatitis. "Razor, if you please."

Razor ripped the card out of the crying man's hand and brought it to him. Bishop set out a piece of copy paper for his lieutenant to set the crumbled and stained business card upon. He'd burn it in the fire the moment he was done with Greeve.

Bishop used his letter opener to move the card around so that he could read it. *Shit.* "A cop?"

"Yeah. Along with some other guy demanding Joey's belongings. They gave me legal papers and threatened me," Greeve explained. "They took my picture."

"Did you allow them to retrieve Joey's belongings?"

"Yeah. I had no choice."

"What were my instructions?"

"To leave the stuff in his apartment."

"Asshole. I have your building being watched because sooner or later, Joey would have returned. Now he will not have a reason to show up." Bishop snapped his fingers, and the four men picked Greeve up off the floor. "Is there anything else you need to tell me?"

62

"N-no, sir. That's all I gots," Greeves said, frustrating Bishop further with his lack of respect for the English language.

"You meant to say, 'That is all you have to give me.'"

"Yeah, that's what I said." Bishop took a deep breath. The guy was an idiot. He couldn't be trusted not to lead the cops straight to Bishop.

His anger deepened at the thought of having to deal with the LAPD. "Take him down to the cellars."

"Wait. I gave you what you needed to find the guy. I can be useful to you."

"What you did was disobey my direct order, forcing me to involve the LAPD, now that Joey's belongings are gone," he explained. Lifting his chin to Razor, Bishop said, "Do what you want with him, and make sure he can't betray me again."

Greeve's shouts and cries tapered off the deeper down his men went into the cellars until there was blessed silence.

Bishop picked up his cigar and lit it, drawing the smoke into his lungs while continuing to stare down at the innocuous, three-and-a-half-inch by two-inch business card that had wholly fucked up his plans.

He was the head of a vast family-run criminal dynasty. Bishop would find his grandson, to ensure his own son lived.

He tapped the card with the letter opener. "What to do with you, Officer Samuel Webb."

***

Joey woke the next morning to the sound of someone knocking on his bedroom door. He glanced over at the clock on his dresser, confirming it was as early as he thought it was. Only a quarter after five in the morning. Immediately he went on alert, concluding that something had to be wrong.

"Come in," he hollered, and then sat up in his bed.

Finn popped his head in as he routinely did. Curiously, he appeared to be more excited than scared or worried. Whatever had happened, it couldn't have been too bad.

"I'm sorry to bug you so early, but I couldn't wait any longer. Miguel came home last night and threatened to tie me to our bed if I came over here before eight. Now don't get me wrong, in certain instances it can be quite fun and eye-opening, but not in this case. I waited until he was in the shower, then I made a break for it and headed straight over," Finn explained before his expression altered a bit. "Do you want me to come back later?"

"After a story like that, fuck no. Get in here," Joey instructed while trying to contain his own laughter so he wouldn't wake the rest of the hub. "What's going on?"

Finn looked back down the hallway, no doubt checking for Miguel, before walking in. He was carrying a medium-size canvas bag over his shoulder that reminded Joey of the same one Marian had brought to the hospital on the day he'd been discharged.

"I have a few things for you I'm positive you're going to love."

Joey could feel Finn's excitement from across the room, and he hated himself for having to ruin the kind gesture. "No, I can't accept whatever you brought. All of you have already given me so much. More than I could have ever dreamed of."

There was no way Joey could take one more gift from his friends, and that's how he viewed this situation, as precious gifts. They'd opened their home and lives to him; that was more than anyone else had ever done.

"I respect that, so, fortunately, the items belonged to you in the first place," Finn said, and then began pulling his treasures out of the bag.

Joey could hear and feel his heart rate speeding up as the first of his treasures touched his shaking hands. Her long blonde hair was dancing in the wind in this picture. They had been on a sunny beach in Santa Monica. His mom had been vivacious and teeming with life right up until her death.

When he looked up, Finn was holding a thin gold chain between his fingers with his mother's locket still attached. Joey's vision blurred. The feeling was indescribable as the small piece of metal slid onto the palm of his hand. In his heart, her jewelry was far dearer to him than any street price could ever match. His tears fell freely, only this time due to happiness and relief.

Joey took the items and held them to his chest. "I—I…" He had to stop and take a few deep breaths before continuing. "I don't know what to say, Finn. There aren't enough words to describe how grateful I am to you. How did you manage to get these out of my old apartment?"

"See right there, I knew I'd end up convincing you to use my first name." He laughed. "I had help." He waggled his brows. "Tall, muscled help. By the way, Greeve is a grade-A asshole."

The name alone caused Joey to have waves of nausea. His super made the johns who frequented certain street corners of the city look like pillars of society. The revolting excuse for a human being had even suggested a way that Joey could help lower his rent.

"I agree with you, he's revolting. Which of the crew went with you? Miguel, Saint, or Max? Oh, wait, was it James?" he asked. "No, it doesn't matter. I'll thank them all." Joey felt like he could fly.

"Nope. It wasn't any of them, though they would have if they could have gotten away from The Gates. Sam's the one who offered to come along with me, which was fortunate because, without him, I don't believe your moron of a super would've let me anywhere near your apartment."

Joey shouldn't be surprised. Sam, son of movie stars, had become a cop. That kinda said it all. "What happened when the two of you confronted Greeve?"

"Once I was able to get over the stench and smoke, I recognized him as a predator. He showed his true colors when two women walked by on their way to their apartment. Thankfully, Sam was ready in case Greeve tried anything. One thing I can say with absolute certainty is that there are parts of that horrible man I never want to see again," Finn explained. "Then he and Sam got into it over your belongings."

"Got into it. Did Sam get hurt?" If he'd had been hurt because of him, Joey would never forgive himself.

"No, no, he's fine," Finn said while waving his hands into the air. "It never came to blows mainly because your man was so many moves ahead of that idiot he wasn't even on the same chessboard." Finn sat down beside him. "Honestly, I don't think I could have gotten in without him."

Joey could see that Finn firmly believed what he was saying. However, one point stood out above the others. "My man?" Joey questioned. "Sam's my friend."

"Come on, who do you think you're trying to fool?" he asked while shaking his head. "I realize he made a terrible mistake last week, and I'm not trying to make light of it, but isn't Sam worthy of a second chance? He's head over heels for you."

"Me?" He was down to using single syllables while his mind spun in a million different directions. Joey couldn't lie. He was attracted to Sam. Who wouldn't be? Kind, intelligent, and handsome: he was the whole package. "That can't be right. Why would he?"

Finn sat down on the edge of his bed and took hold of Joey's sweaty hand. "Joey, the real question here is, why do you think he wouldn't be? You're funny, smart, compassionate, and adorable."

That's a laundry list of qualities he hadn't heard in a long time. "Adorable? I don't believe that's as flattering as you think it is."

"Let's see. You're charming, attractive, and lovable. I can pull up a dictionary if you want proof," Finn said, bringing his cell phone forward and waving it. "Trust me, you… are… adorable."

"It doesn't matter." Joey looked away, knowing he had a point to make. "There can never be anything romantic between Sam and me. That's a hard no."

"Why?" Finn asked, looking honestly confused.

Joey slouched back against his headboard and took a deep breath. He wasn't confident he could say this more than once. "Isn't it obvious? I'm sick. I'm going to probably die in the next fifteen years. Sam has to find someone wonderful that he can love and grow old with, not a man who's in and out of hospitals, or who's so bone-deep tired at times that he has to struggle to get out of bed. Sam is incredible, and he needs, no, deserves a person with a future."

"Really? So you think you know what I deserve?" The question came from across the room through the open doorway where Sam and Miguel now stood. "I'll tell you what I need. It's you."

Finn stood up, headed to the door, and left with no good-byes. He closed the door behind him, leaving Sam alone with Joey, who had been so surprised he'd been struck speechless.

"And here I wasn't going to push you. I promised the crew I wouldn't, but hearing you say those words about us cuts deeper than any physical injury ever could," Sam said, before walking over to the side of his bed and sitting down. "I have a say in this, too."

"Sam, it's…."

"What, true? Yes, I care about you and want the opportunity to get to know you, and not in the friend zone. I want to be by your side through whatever happens next."

"Sweet, but impractical." The words were hard to get out. They scraped and clawed his throat in an attempt to stop him from speaking the truth. "You don't know the truth." He felt that tingling sensation in the tip of his nose that portending tears. "I can't give you the life you've earned surviving a nightmarish childhood. A long, happy life. Someone to come home to who is well, not stretched out in bed, sleeping off another health crisis. You need someone to make plans with and argue with about where the two of you will retire. Sam, I'm battling sickle cell disease. I don't have a lifetime left to offer you."

There wasn't a single moment in Joey's life that he'd hated his disease more than right now. Did he want Sam to be with somebody else? Hell no. But he couldn't bear to be with him for a few years and then leave him behind to suffer.

"Move over," Sam ordered as he stood up from the chair. "I need to hold you."

Joey's body moved on its own accord. Eager to get closer to the one man his soul ached to have while forcing himself to push that same man as far away as possible. He was at war with himself, as his body had always been: his own worst enemy.

Without saying another word, Sam shoved his boots off and climbed in under the thick covers. Joey liked to be warm when he slept. It comforted him, and, frankly, he needed it. In one fluid motion, Sam wrapped him in his strong arms and gently pulled Joey closer, until he was flush against Sam's more substantial body, and his head rested on the big guy's chest.

Joey didn't even bother putting up a fight. With his emotions swirling, he needed an anchor, and there was no other place he'd rather be.

"I'm sorry you're sick. I truly am. But if you think for one second that that's going to scare me away, you're wrong," Sam said. "I'll be honest, I don't know much about the disease, but I'll learn."

"You're not going to like what you find." Joey still had some fight left in him, but it was dissolving as he enjoyed the comfort of being warm and snug in Sam's arms.

"You're going to have to let me be the judge of that," Sam said. "For right now, we're going to take a nap and get up at a more decent hour. From this point on, you're not getting rid of me. Provided you want me too?"

His head popped up off Sam's chest so quickly that it spun for a few seconds. "How could I not? You're remarkable."

"I feel the same way about you," he confirmed while running his thumb along Joey's jawline, making him lose track of their conversation. Sam's rough hands were gentle when they touched him. "I don't care how long it takes me to convince you of that, but I swear you're going to believe it yourself someday."

They both lay quietly for a few minutes, Joey listening to Sam's steady heartbeat, and then something occurred to him. "Sam."

"Yeah," he replied in a deep, sleepy voice that vibrated through his chest.

"Why are you here so early?"

Sam drew him closer and said, "I had a meeting to attend at the station. When I was leaving, I saw Miguel come racing down the street to The Gates. Unsure what was going on, I raced after him in case there was any trouble."

"Yeah, trouble has a name. Finn. The stuff at the station, I hope it wasn't anything too serious. You okay?"

"It wasn't anything terrible, and yes, I'm good. A body turned up in an alley west of Skid Row around midnight."

"That's terrible, you said it wasn't."

"Some would say it was a blessing," Sam remarked. "Now, lie down and go to sleep."

He yawned wide before cozying down to attempt to get some more sleep. Joey wasn't exactly sure how he was going to accomplish that with Sam pressed up against him, but it wasn't too long before his eyelids grew heavy.

As Joey fell asleep, he swore he heard Sam say, "I'm keeping you."

Chapter Eight

Sam sat in his cruiser, upset he hadn't told Joey the truth. He'd kept the details of the dumped body to himself, figuring that now wasn't the time to share that Greeve was the dead guy. Someone had worked him over, and good, but according to the coroner, the cause of death was a heart attack. He could see it happening. The man wasn't the poster boy for good health weekly, then add in some severe stressors—knives, iron knuckles, and tire irons—and his heart was bound to give out.

After he and Finn had come back from Joey's apartment, Sam had given the crew a heads-up in case there was any blowback from Greeve. Though he didn't like a murder in his sector, Sam couldn't say he was sorry the asshole was dead.

Sam cracked the driver's side window of his cruiser to let in the cool night air. So far, Ross hadn't been able to dig up any leads on the Greeve murder. For all Sam knew the death was caused by a deal gone wrong. Hell, maybe he owed someone money, or the tenants banded together to get rid of the POS. All were possible scenarios. However, Sam wasn't buying any of them, and neither was Detective Ross.

The two of them had an early morning meeting with the captain after the body was extricated from a Dumpster in an alley behind an old diner. Ross had been assigned to the case, and when he realized Greeve was the same man Sam had paid a visit to the previous afternoon, he'd called Sam in. The three of them had spent some time going over what they knew. Other than a rumor that Bishop Venzezo, the local mob boss, was responsible, they had nothing to go on. Ross couldn't arrest someone on hearsay. They needed substantial evidence. Especially when it came to Venzezo, the slippery bastard. Over a dozen arrests and none of them ever got to the charging stage. To take down a mob boss, the evidence had to be airtight and considerable.

Ross was professionally and personally driven to find something that pointed at Bishop, but as of yet, nothing. Ross and his partner James were involved in a case not too long ago that included Avante, one of Bishop's associates, who was responsible for the detective ending up in the hospital.

The moment the captain heard Bishop's name, he assigned two more detectives to the case. Anything involving that psycho Venzezo demanded all hands on deck. There were few photos of Venzezo, and what they had on file were blurry, a side view, or too far away to make a positive ID. The man wanted to remain a ghost and, for the most part, was succeeding.

Sam tried but couldn't shake the feeling that Greeve's death had something to do with their visit to pick up Joey's belongings. He didn't have a stitch of proof, but his instincts had him double-checking his mirrors as he drove down South Broadway. Sure enough, the same vehicle he'd spotted earlier was still hanging far enough back that he couldn't read the plate and run it. Occasionally cars would switch out, but he wasn't fooled. Who would want to follow a cop? If someone wanted his attention, this was the right way of going about it.

Sam activated his radio and called dispatch, reciting the LAPD code indicating that he was being followed.

Fed up, he was getting ready to turn his cruiser around and activate his lights when the distinct sound of a gunshot, followed by the spidering of the glass in his rear window, had him pressing harder on his accelerator. Sure enough, two of the four gunmen in the car behind him were hanging out of the windows, firing off shots at him. What the hell?

Picking up speed, he called for assistance.

His radio crackled to life, and he gave his location and dispatch kept the channel open, letting him know backup was right behind him.

He ignored the chatter on the radio and concentrated on the road. His speedometer read over eighty mph and still climbing, but he couldn't shake the gunmen.

Repeated bullet impacts to the body of his cruiser pushed him to drive even faster. Firing guns on the streets of LA guaranteed someone innocent was going to be hurt. These men weren't giving up, and they didn't care who they hit.

Sam took a hard right, causing the back end of his cruiser to drift left. Luckily he was able to pull his vehicle back under control and decided he had to get out of DTLA and to somewhere empty of potential casualties. He told dispatch he was heading to Dodger Stadium. There wasn't a game scheduled, and the parking lots would be deserted.

He turned onto Stadium Way and flew into Lot One parking. There was no chance of him returning fire and still maintaining control of his speeding cruiser, no matter what the movies portrayed. Instead, he weaved and dodged around light pillars and between a few outbuildings, anything to throw off his pursuers' aim.

He'd changed direction, and pain exploded from his left arm, halfway between his shoulder and elbow. Sam didn't have the time to look at the damage because the assholes were catching up with him. His arm hung limp against his side, and he told dispatch he was injured. Thankfully, he saw lights flashing in the distance. His backup was racing in from the opposite end of the parking lot.

Six cars were speeding toward him, so he floored the gas pedal and buried the needle. All that time praying he didn't lose control of his vehicle since he only had one working arm.

Several more shots rang out. Sam was less than one hundred yards away from the other cruisers when the suspects slammed on their brakes. It would be too late for them to get away as Sam watched more cruisers pulling into the lot behind them.

The row of vehicles ahead of him split down the center, allowing Sam to continue past them to safety. Shots continued to volley as he brought his cruiser to a stop and turned around. By now, his police brothers and sisters had the four suspects face down on the ground. One of the four wasn't moving.

The adrenaline racing through his body helped to numb a large portion of his pain. Sam finally had the chance to look down at his lifeless arm. A pool of blood had already begun dripping from his seat and onto the floor of the cruiser. Reaching for his radio took much more effort than it usually did as his head began to swim and he told dispatch where he was and his condition.

His vision pulsed in and out as more chatter broke out over the radio. Sam could make out two sets of lights heading his way, or it could have been four sets. His world was spinning even faster, and his vision became blurry. He knew he wouldn't be conscious when help arrived.

***

Agonizing. That summed up sitting in the surgical floor waiting room, hoping for word on Sam's condition. Alongside him were members of the LAPD and the entire Gates crew. Over six hours had passed since Sam was taken into emergency surgery, and they'd heard nothing since. The only bit of information Joey knew was that Sam had lost a large amount of blood.

Saint had been a godsend. A former surgeon, he'd spoken to the attending physician in the ER, and was able to provide enough information so that the packed ER waiting room was briefed as to Sam's condition. While Saint said Sam would be fine, Joey hadn't felt better. Most of the group migrated to the surgery floor. Only a few cops had left after the brass got a status report.

"He'll be fine. Sam's tough," Ross said as he placed his hand on Joey's shoulder. "He'll be pissed that he's going to be off the job for a while."

Joey nodded. Speaking took too much effort. He was having a difficult time waiting for an update on Sam's condition. He'd paced around the room so many times he'd lost count of how many laps he'd done.

Marian had to convince him to sit down to eat and rest. He'd be of no use to Sam if he ended up in a hospital bed alongside him.

Two men walked in, and Ross got up to talk with them. Maybe they'd uncovered who did this and why. Joey didn't care about any of that right now. All he wanted was for Sam to survive. Nothing else mattered. His own self-doubts and fears took a backseat now that reality came knocking, and broke down the door when a tall doctor walked into the room with his head down, concentrating on the tablet in his hand, and causing the entire room to stand. "Officer Samuel Webb?" the doctor asked before looking up to see the place packed with officers. "Ah, I see."

Ross stepped away from the men he'd been talking with and approached the doctor. "I'm Detective Ross, how is he?"

Joey's body began to shake, and Finn and Miguel came to stand beside him, each with a hand on his shoulder.

"The surgery went well. He's out of recovery and is in his room resting. We were able to stop the bleeding, and he's got a few pins holding his shoulder in place while the bones knit."

"So he's out of danger?" Joey asked.

The doctor's expression changed from clinical to compassionate when he looked over at Joey. "Yes. He's going to be fine."

Joey almost collapsed, and he would have if Miguel and Finn hadn't been there to hold him up. Relief rushed over him. Sam was going to live. He wasn't going to lose the man he loved. Joey's brain ground to a stop. Love? They'd met a little over a month ago. How could he love him?

Before Joey had the chance to get a handle on himself, Ross was calling for him. "Come on, Joey, Sam's waiting."

Joey snapped out of it and joined Ross. The doctor led the two of them down a few corridors before stopping in front of a room. "He has a long way to go, and PT is a must, but I expect Sam will be able to make a full recovery."

"Thank you," Joey said.

"You're welcome," he answered.

The doctor walked over to the nurses' station, and Joey reached for the door handle. His heart was racing. Sam was alive and behind this door.

He tried to make as little noise as possible in case Sam was sleeping. When Joey pulled the curtain back, Sam was wide awake, propped in his bed. His smile was the catalyst, and those tears Joey had been fighting came pouring down.

Sam opened his uninjured arm. "I'm okay. Come here, Joey."

Joey tried to wipe away his tears before reaching Sam, but they wouldn't stop coming. Sam wrapped his arm around Joey's waist and lifted him up onto the bed.

"You shouldn't be doing that. Something could happen," Joey admonished while trying to stop him.

"This arm is working just fine," Sam said while pulling Joey closer. "Lie down, honey."

Joey didn't have to be asked twice and lowered his head to rest on the right side of Sam's broad chest. His usual earthy scent of sandalwood still came through amid the smell of antiseptic. Joey buried his face against Sam's chest, finally understanding that life was already too short even without illness. He was determined to share as much of his love for as long as he had left.

"How are you feeling?" Ross asked Sam. Joey didn't even bother looking up. He wasn't moving from his spot.

"Like I've been shot. What'd you think?" Sam chuckled. "I'm going to be fine. The doctor said I need some downtime and PT, then I'll be able to return to work."

"Good to hear. You have a whole room full of people waiting on word that you'd made it through surgery."

Joey couldn't help but tense.

"I'm fine," Sam said as he kissed the top of Joey's head. "Nothing more to worry about, all the stress is over. I don't want you getting sick."

Joey agreed that was not what he wanted to have happen and nodded.

"Any news on what those men wanted other than to kill me?"

"The suspects have given us nothing and lawyered up, but we know who they work for."

"Who?"

"Bishop Venzezo."

Joey bolted off the bed and growled, "I'll kill that old man with my bare hands."

Both Sam and Ross looked at him in shock and were watching him closely. "Joey, honey. What's going on?" Sam asked.

Joey's anger dissipated enough for him to realize what he'd done. *Shit.* It didn't matter now who knew what. His grandfather was trying to kill the man Joey loved. He had to come clean and hope they understood.

"What is it?" Ross asked.

Joey squared his shoulders and said, "There's something you need to know, and I'm worried about what might happen when you find out."

"Come here." Sam reached out and took Joey's hand. "We'll figure it out together, remember. You're not alone now."

"Bishop is my estranged grandfather. My mom's father."

Both Sam and Ross were silent. Precisely what he'd expected, but at least no one was yelling. Joey didn't bother looking at either of them, sure of the disappointment he'd see, but the fact remained, his grandfather had tried to kill Sam, and Joey wouldn't sit by and let it happen again.

"Joey," Sam said while squeezing his hand. "Why didn't you tell me?"

"We haven't seen or spoken to each other in over nineteen years. I'd hoped he was now a nonissue, but I was wrong." He finally looked into Sam's eyes. "I was afraid people would hold what my family has done against me."

Sam once again coaxed Joey back onto the side of his bed. "I understand. Why haven't you had contact with him in so long?"

"We left. My mom wanted me out of his control, and it wasn't as if Granddad cared. His only grandson was diseased, as he liked to put it. He never came looking for us, and eventually, we changed our names and started a new life. I was close to ten years old."

"Tall. You chose that name, didn't you?" Sam asked.

Joey couldn't help but smile at the memory. "My mom and I were trying to decide on new names, I wanted mine to stay as Joey, but a new last name sounded great. There was no way I was going to carry around the Venzezo name. My mom asked me what I thought, and I suggested Tall. We both knew that was the only way I'd ever be *tall*."

Sam smiled and gathered him closer.

"Do you know of any reason your grandfather would want to hurt Sam?" Ross asked. "Maybe this could have something to do with Greeve's death."

"Greeve?" Joey asked.

"That's who we found in the alley," Sam explained.

"Why didn't you tell me?"

"You were recovering and happy to have your mother's belongings back. I couldn't bring myself to ruin that."

"So, Greeve was killed after you and Finn went to see him about my apartment."

"Yeah, and we have a feeling that's not a coincidence."

"What about Finn? He went too. We have to protect him."

"Don't worry, Miguel and the crew are well aware of the situation, and if someone's dumb enough to take Miguel on, they deserve the ass-kicking they're going to get," Sam assured with a grin.

Joey knew that no one would be getting past that Marine. "Did anything strange happen when you were talking to him? There has to be something because if Granddad is this bold, there's a reason."

Sam laid his head back on his pillow, and Joey could tell that he was getting tired.

"The only thing that stood out was when Greeve read the letter from Saint's lawyer demanding entrance to your apartment. Greeve seemed shocked and a bit worried when he realized we were there for your stuff. I think his exact words were, 'What is it with this kid?' When I asked him why he'd said that, Greeve shoved the key to your apartment into my hands and slammed the door on us."

"I wonder what he meant." Joey thought it odd Greeve cared enough to say anything.

"Also, before we even got into the building, a man came storming out. A scar on the side of his face, an expensive suit, got into a red sports car. I've been wondering if he'd paid a visit to Greeve, but I've found no solid connection."

Scar? Couldn't be. He never did his own dirty work.

Ross was busy on his cell phone, and Joey took the opportunity to apologize. "I'm sorry I didn't tell you, especially after how honest you were about your own family."

Sam cupped the side of Joey's face and pulled him closer before kissing him. Every nerve sprang to life as Sam brushed his tongue over the seam of Joey's lips, coaxing them to open so that he could explore farther inside.

The sound of someone clearing his throat brought Joey back to the hospital room. They were in a hospital bed, in front of Ross, sharing their first kiss. Not how he thought it would play out, but Joey didn't care.

Sam slowed the kiss, rubbing the tip of his nose against Joey's before turning to look back at Ross. "Yeah?"

Ross turned the screen on his phone to face them and said, "Do you recognize him?"

Joey stared unblinking at the face of a killer. He knew that scar and how it got there.

Sam responded first. "That's the man who was coming out of Joey's apartment. Who is it?"

"My grandfather," Joey admitted flatly. His hope that this had nothing to do with him had disappeared.

"Okay, that's enough for now. I need to rest," Sam said, and Joey shifted his body to slide back off the bed. "Where are you going?"

"You said you needed to rest."

"I do, but I want to do it with you. Ross has a lot of digging ahead of him, now that he has this new information."

"What do you think the crew will say when they find out who I am?" He felt sick at the thought of losing them from his life.

"Nothing hurtful about you, I'm positive. None of this is your fault, and it's understandable why you weren't too willing to share that information. Now when it comes to Bishop, yeah, there's going to be some anger. He's messed in a lot of people's lives."

Joey nodded again. He understood that anger. He had plenty of his own. They'd have to wait and see how it all played out, but for right now, Joey slid off his running shoes and crawled back up onto the bed and lay down beside Sam. "Are you sure it's okay for me to stay here with you? I don't want to leave you, but if it causes a problem..."

"I'll make sure of it," Ross replied. "Then I'll ask Finn if he can bring some clothes over for you because Sam's going to be in here for a few days."

Joey looked up the bed at Sam, who was already asleep. He needed as much rest as possible to heal, and Joey would make sure of it.

"Thank you, Ross."

"No worries, Joey. And, hey, remember, you're not your grandfather." Ross walked out of the room, leaving Joey to run any and all possible reasons for his grandfather to be interested in him after all this time, and to have people killed and shooting at a cop, at Sam. What the hell was going on?

Joey snuggled up against Sam's side and pulled the covers up over them. The only thing that mattered right now was the man in this bed.

Joey would protect Sam from his grandfather no matter what he had to do.

Chapter Nine

"What do you mean, there's nothing more you can do?" Bishop growled at his private doctor. "We need more time."

"Sir, we've done everything we can. If Luca doesn't get a kidney transplant, he won't live to the end of the month. There are no available organ donors compatible with your son, and we've exhausted all other, shall we say, less than scrupulous avenues."

Bishop slammed his tablet back down onto his desk, shattering the screen and leaving a few superficial cuts on his hand. "Our best chance is a relative, that's what you said."

"Yes, sir, but we've tested you and your family members and couldn't find anyone who matches."

"You've tested all but one family member," Bishop explained. "There's one more we're still trying to locate. I've given you his medical records, and his blood type matches my son's."

"We've told you the likelihood this donor is viable is slim given his illness. They'll have to be found soon to do more testing. Your son could go into acute renal failure at any time."

"I'll get you your kidney. Get out."

Without another word, the doctor left, closing the study door behind him. Bishop stormed across the room to his well-stocked bar, grabbed a bottle of scotch and a tumbler, before bringing them both back to his desk.

He gave himself a long pour, then drank half the tumbler's contents down before setting the bottle on his desk. Bishop absently ran the tips of his fingers down the thick line cut into the left side of his face.

"I'll find you, Joey, and then I can repay for this," Bishop promised. "Your mother and grandmother are no longer around to protect you."

The only part of his plan that Bishop felt even a twang of regret over was the fact that the kidney would have to be removed from

Joey far too quickly to save Luca's life. Leaving Bishop without the time to repay his grandson in the most painful of ways possible.

**

Joey had spent all morning cleaning to make sure his room was spotless, even though it hadn't been a mess or dirty to begin with. He wanted the place to be perfect for when Sam arrived. It had been decided he would recover here in the hub where there were people to help him and keep an eye on him. Sam would be moving into this bedroom with Joey.

Four days had passed since the shooting, and the big guy was chomping at the bit to get out of the hospital. Sam would have to keep his arm in a sling for the foreseeable future, but he was alive and coming home, and that was all that mattered.

Joey had spent time setting up the gaming system in front of his television on an angle that ensured the box wouldn't interfere with the view of the game. He'd ordered two new racing games off the Internet with Finn's help. He realized that Sam wasn't bedbound, but he'd have to rest if he wanted to get better.

Joey took one last scan of his bedroom and bathroom, double-checking that everything was ready, picked up a small bag of garbage from the floor, and headed out to the Dumpster. Ross would be picking Sam up and driving him over to The Gates while Joey prepared.

The rest of the crew was working or occupied with the restaurant and lounge in the front of the house. Joey walked through the hub on his way to the back door, and sure enough, it was empty. He found himself humming, actually humming. He was happier, healthier, and mostly pain-free for the past two days.

Once he walked through the maze of shelves holding stock, he came to the reinforced steel back door. Joey placed the palm of his hand on the scanning pad built into the wall. Saint had to have spent a fortune installing the security system at The Gates. There wasn't a key per se; all those who had access to the hub had their palm prints saved in the system to gain access through the back of the building

As he watched, the glowing green line ran up and down his palm. Joey almost felt as though he was in some futuristic, adventure-spy movie. He couldn't help but laugh at himself. Although, when he stopped to think about it, he realized that now every day felt like a new adventure for him.

New worlds were opening up, and he was ready to explore it all: new experiences, new feelings, safety, security, friendship, and Sam. For the first time in his life, since his mom had left him, Joey felt happy. Not only the happy persona he carried around like an old coat to ensure no one had a reason to look underneath, but sincerely happy down deep inside of him.

The only thing left for him to do was to uncover what his grandfather was after and stop him. Then Joey could begin this new life, no matter how many years he had left. As long as he stayed right here with Sam by his side, he swore to embrace each day instead of dreading it and live each one to the fullest.

Joey would write the end of his own story the way he chose, and when the time came, there would be memories left behind with his friends and the man he loved. Joey would never truly disappear as if he never existed.

Speaking of the man he loved, Joey had to get a move on if he wanted to be ready in time. Joey wondered when he'd be brave enough to tell Sam that he was in love with him. The more time Joey had to think about it, the more real it became. He loved Sam.

The scanner flashed green, and he heard the locks turning. Joey opened the door and stepped out into the gorgeous afternoon sun. The day had turned out to be bright and warm, even with the news predicting rain. He soaked in the warm rays as he slowly walked down the stairs and over to the Dumpster.

While he was throwing away the bag of garbage, he was scanning the area. Joey knew what it felt like to be watched. There were eyes on him right now from somewhere close by, although he couldn't pick anything out of the ordinary from his surroundings.

The cars parked on the street were all empty, and he couldn't find a sign or shadow of anyone looking down from any of the windows. Those facts didn't matter. Joey's gut told him that someone was out there. He turned and walked back to the staircase as quickly as he could. When he'd almost reached the top step, he heard someone coming up behind him.

"Hey, Joey, how's it going."

On instinct, Joey spun around, fists raised, prepared to fight as hard as he could. No one was going to fuck up his happy new life.

Especially his vile grandfather. Joey swung with his right fist moments before realizing it was Brad standing behind him. Fortunately, Brad had fast reflexes and ducked out of the way in time.

"Whoa," Brad yelled. "What the hell did I do to you?"

Joey pulled his arms back away from the bartender, who looked to be reporting for duty. Staff would have to ring the buzzer to have someone come let them in. They didn't have access to the back of the building.

"I'm sorry," Joey said. "I got freaked out, I guess."

"Yeah, well, I shouldn't have come up behind you like that either," Brad said while shaking out his arms. "It would have scared anybody."

Joey's initial assessment of Brad had changed over time. The guy was cautious and watchful: so was Joey. Brad had fit in well at The Gates and turned out to be one of the hardest workers they had.

"I'm a little jumpy, that's all. Come on, I'll let you in."

Brad was busy scanning the area much the same way as he always seemed to do. "You sure you're okay?"

Joey felt terrible for almost punching Brad, especially now that the man looked worried about him. "Yes, thank you for your concern. I guess with all that's been going on around me lately, I've let my imagination get carried away."

"If you say so, but if you don't mind me making a suggestion. Maybe it would be safer if you didn't come out back alone."

"Duly noted." Joey agreed that sounded like a good idea.

The two finished climbing the stairs, and Joey unlocked the door with his palm scan. Brad went in toward the staff breakroom, but Joey waited and took one last look around. Whatever had him spooked was gone, and it no longer felt as though someone was watching him. Brad had a valid point. Until this thing with his grandfather was over, Joey needed to be more cautious. With a thug like Bishop, you were never sure where he'd show up.

***

Sam walked into the hub alongside Ross and Saint. The two were carrying his bags, reminding him that the doctor advised Sam to take it easy. He still had one good arm left, but apparently, no one wanted him to use it.

Before he could ask where his love was, Joey came running into the central living room and straight up to Sam. He opened his arm, and the adorable man slipped right into his side. Joey fit perfectly.

"How are you feeling? Do you want to sit down?" Joey asked while attempting to lead him over to the couch.

Sam didn't fight it. He knew that Joey needed to take care of him. They'd been through a lot in their short time together, and thankfully, they'd only drawn closer because of it.

"Maybe I'll sit for a bit," Sam said.

He was having a difficult time picking out a memory of when he'd received this type of attention at home, even when he was sick or hurt.

He had to admit that his arm was aching, but Sam wasn't taking any more painkillers. They brought back bad memories, and he wanted nothing to do with them. Of course, he understood that in this case, narcotics were necessary for the short term. But, unlike Joey, Sam wasn't experiencing chronic debilitating pain. A couple of over-the-counter pain medication was all he needed. Besides, the drugs made him sluggish and his brain cloudy, two things he hated, especially when there was someone out to kill him.

"Of course, sit right here. I'll get you a bottle of water," Joey instructed as he walked toward the kitchen.

"Joey's going to be like this for a while if he's anything like my James was when I was hurt. Good luck." Ross laughed and dropped Sam's bag down beside the couch. "He acted as if I was made out of glass."

"It'll take him time to feel safe again instead of living in fear of possibly losing you," Saint explained.

"I understand," Sam said. "Joey's in control through my recovery." By allowing Joey to hover, Sam hoped it would help Joey recover from the shock and stress of the shooting.

Joey came back into the room, carrying a bottle of water and a sandwich. He set the plate down on the coffee table in front of Sam and handed him the water. "In case you're hungry. Hospital food sucks. I should know."

Sam had been smiling so often recently that his cheeks hurt. He couldn't think of a way to explain how he'd come to love Joey, but he did. He swore to spend every moment of their time together showing him.

After Joey set the napkin down beside the plate, Sam reached for him and waited until Joey settled in close before taking a swallow of water. "That's better."

Joey looked up at him with those big blue eyes and said, "Much better," before cuddling in close to Sam's side.

"Do you have any news on the Bishop front?" Saint asked while sitting down on a chair opposite the coffee table. Ross joined them.

"Yes and no," Ross answered.

"Okay?" Sam knew that the answer wasn't going to fly. "Care to throw some specifics in there, Detective?"

"Right. We have more information, but no, we don't have enough proof to move forward. So far, our informants are telling us that the streets are teeming with rumors about Bishop. Some say he's searching for someone important, while others say that he's lost his edge since his son got sick, and that the sharks are circling waiting for one slip."

Joey sat up so quickly that Sam had to hold on to his arm so he didn't fall off the couch. "Son? What son?"

Ross looked confused for a moment. "You didn't know Bishop had a son?"

"No. There was no son around when my mother and I lived with him. It had been only the three of us."

"You haven't heard from him in over nineteen years, this could have happened after your mom took you away," Sam explained. "In fact, I've never heard about him having a son until now. It's not common knowledge."

"Does this mean I have an uncle?" Joey asked. "I'm not sure I should be happy or concerned."

"Luca Venzezo is your uncle, and if he's anything like your grandfather, I wouldn't go looking for a family reunion," Ross warned. "There's isn't much known about him, other than the fact that he's sick."

"Does he have sickle cell disease?"

"I don't know for sure," Ross answered. "Your mom must have been carrying the sickle cell trait, and your dad as well, but do you know if your grandfather is a carrier?"

"I don't think he is. The fact that I had the disease was shameful enough to the family name. Venzezos are supposed to be powerful and strong, and I had no hope of ever fitting that mold. He liked to punish me for being such a disappointment." Joey's expression changed from concern to sadness in a heartbeat. "He used to punish my mom, too. Funny, the bastard probably went out to create his own heir after his daughter produced a failure only to find out his son was sick as well."

Sam sat up and gathered Joey's shaking body against his side. "It's going to be okay, honey. You never have to worry about any of that ever happening again. I wish you hadn't had to live through it at all. He's an evil man plain and simple. None of this is your fault."

Joey laid his head on Sam's shoulder. "Are there any other rumors floating around?"

Ross pulled out his notepad and rifled through the first few pages. "Not really, only that Bishop's men have been combing the streets for the last week trying to find someone."

"Do you think it's me?" Joey asked without looking up.

Sam wouldn't lie to him. "It could be. We're prepared to protect you, don't worry."

"What about you?" Joey asked. "He came after you. He tried to kill you."

"You're both going to be protected," Ross said. "We have cruisers sitting out on the streets and uniformed bicycle officers making rounds in the area. I don't know what Bishop wants, but I won't risk him getting to either of you. With the extra security already installed here at The Gates, they won't be able to walk right in."

Sam had respected Detective Ross since meeting him years ago, but his protective streak was impressive, and it made him wonder if his partner, James, was actually the more protective one in their relationship.

"Okay, keep me in the loop. Now I have to get back to the restaurant. If you need anything, call," Saint said before standing and leaving the hub, heading in the direction of the central kitchen.

Joey reached out and picked up the plate. "You should eat a bit to keep your strength up."

Sam would do whatever Joey wanted. He picked up half the sandwich with his uninjured right hand and dug in.

"Yeah, I gotta get back to the station," Ross announced as he stood. "I'll let you know if I hear anything."

"Thanks, Ross," Sam said.

"Thank you so much," Joey said while holding out his hand for the detective to shake. "I appreciate everything you're doing for us."

Ross smiled and shook Joey's hand. "Try not to worry too much and stress yourself. You need to take care of Sam."

"I will. Promise."

"Good. I'll touch base with you guys tomorrow."

Moments later, Sam and Joey were alone, for which Sam was grateful. It had been a whirlwind since the shooting, and all Sam wanted to do now was hold Joey in his arms.

"How about we go get me settled into our room," Sam suggested.

"I'd like that," Joey agreed before standing. He grunted as he tried to pick up one of the two heavy bags.

"Don't worry about those, babe, I can move them."

"You will not. You need to rest, the doctor's instructions were clear. I'm strong enough to carry them for you."

He wanted to argue but held himself in check. Joey needed this, and no matter what Sam said, his love wouldn't accept it.

"Okay, but I'm carrying the other bag." Before he had a chance to argue, Sam picked up his duffle using his right arm and headed for the hallway. He still couldn't let Joey overdo it and exhaust himself straight back into the hospital.

"I'll grab your sandwich," Joey replied before following Sam down the hallway and into their room.

Sam hadn't shared his plans with Joey, but he didn't intend to sleep without Joey by his side from this day forward. He would go anywhere his love was, even if he had to sell his condo to do it. Sam had come to some important life decisions lying in that hospital bed. Now it was time to implement a few.

He set his bag down on a chair and looked around the room. He didn't miss the gaming setup Joey had prepared for him, and Sam's heart melted. "I see someone's looking for a rematch."

Joey's cheeks turned a beautiful shade of red. "I wanted you to feel comfortable here. Finn helped me pick out a couple new racing games for you."

Sam walked over to the stack and picked up the two games still wrapped in their plastic covering. Had he ever had someone do something specifically for him, just to make him happy?

"If you don't like them, I can return them, and you can pick new ones," Joey offered, and Sam could hear his uncertainty.

Sam spun around and pulled Joey into his arm. "You're amazing. What I ever did to deserve you is a mystery, but I'm thankful every damn day that I did it."

He lowered his head and took possession of Joey's soft lips. He tasted sweet, almost like honey, and Sam wanted more. Joey's soft moans drove the kiss deeper, their tongues dueling as Sam began to harden in his jeans. The passion between the two of them was off the charts, but Sam had to show some restraint. He slowed their kiss until both of them were standing inches apart, breathing as if they'd run a hundred-meter sprint.

Joey's eyes shined even bright as he looked up at Sam. "You are so beautiful, love." His expression changed slightly, and Sam realized what he'd said, but he wasn't taking it back. Joey deserved to know, and if he needed more time to express his feelings, Sam was prepared to wait as long as it took.

"Love?" Joey asked. "You love me?"

Running his thumb over Joey's kiss-swollen lips almost drew him in for another kiss. "Yeah. I love you."

Joey looked stunned for a moment. "I thought it was only me."

"Only you?" Sam asked. "Right. I love only you."

"No, I meant, I love you too. I've been keeping it to myself because I didn't want to pressure you into feeling the same way." Joey nervously picked at the imaginary fluff on the front of Sam's shirt.

"There's no pressure, only love, Joey," Sam confirmed. "Why don't we get changed into some comfortable clothing and give these new games a test run." He knew Joey wouldn't appreciate making a big deal out of their declarations of love. It was a new feeling for both of them.

Joey's smile seemed to brighten the entire room. "I'll help you unpack your stuff."

"Thanks, honey," Sam replied before taking one more quick kiss. "Oh, and I picked this up for you." He reached into his bag, pulled out a new cell phone, and handed it to Joey. "Now we can always reach one another. All the information and phone number are in the box, and I've already saved my number. All you have to do is press my picture on your home screen."

"Thank you," Joey said with a hitch in his voice. "You think of everything."

Wanting to reassure Joey and make him more comfortable, he continued. "Don't be thanking me so soon. You'll be sick and tired of my calls in no time."

"Never going to happen," Joey assured while shaking his head side to side.

The two of them spent the next several minutes unpacking Sam's bags and storing his belongings alongside Joey's. A simple thing that made Sam happier than he'd ever thought it would. Together. The two of them were partners, a team, side by side by choice—everything Sam had ever wanted.

Chapter Ten

Joey rolled over and draped his arm over Sam's hard stomach. Even with him still being asleep, Sam's right arm was wrapped around him. The man never ceased to make Joey feel loved and wanted. It had been four days since they'd become roommates and boyfriends.

Every morning Joey had a moment of panic, afraid that it had all been a dream. Until he reached over and confirmed that Sam was lying in bed beside him. He hoped that over time his subconscious would accept that he wasn't alone in the world any longer.

Their connection had grown stronger with each passing day. The two of them had been spending all their time together. They'd talk for hours and play Sam's racing games, and never once did Joey wish to be anywhere else.

In fact, he wanted even more of a physical connection.

They'd explored and made out plenty of times. Honestly, who wouldn't with Sam walking around in a towel? Joey was finding it difficult to keep his hands to himself. He wanted to share so much more with Sam.

In the past, sex had been a need for physical gratification and nothing more. Now that he and Sam loved one another, Joey wanted to share that connection in every possible way. Absently, his fingers traced the outline of Sam's abdominal muscles as he thought of how he should proceed.

"You okay, honey?" Sam's sleep-roughened voice made Joey's cock twitch. He was semi-hard to begin with, which was his perpetual state since Sam's arrival. He couldn't seem to get himself under control.

"I'm fine. Couldn't sleep," Joey answered while slowly moving his hips away from Sam's side. It was embarrassing enough running around with a hard-on in the daytime.

"Where are you going?" Sam asked while holding him closer. There was no way he couldn't feel Joey's dilemma.

"Giving you more room." That sounded lame even to him.

Sam looked down at him with that sexy grin in place and said, "Room isn't what I need."

He was almost afraid to ask in case Sam didn't want the same thing Joey wanted. "What do you need?"

His grip tightened around Joey's waist. "For us to make love."

A troop of hummingbirds took flight inside Joey's stomach as he watched Sam's gaze turn heated. "Me too, but what about your arm?"

Sam shifted his hard body so that they were now fully facing one another. "One arm won't be a problem. Do we have supplies?"

Joey could feel his cheeks warming but nodded his head anyway. "I ordered a few things."

"Did Finn help you this time?" Sam asked, smiling as he raised a single eyebrow.

"No, I figured it all out on my own."

"Next time we'll do it together. Do some browsing while we're at it."

Joey couldn't help his soft groan. This man was too sexy for his own good.

"Come here, honey," Sam crooned.

Joey lifted himself up to hover over Sam, leaving their lips less than an inch apart and said, "I love you, Samuel Webb, completely. Not a doubt in my mind."

"Good, because someday I'm going to get you to marry me," Sam said before closing the distance and taking command of Joey's lips.

Joey moaned. He couldn't stop himself. His body burned with the need to get closer. Sam had on only a pair of boxers, which were easy for Joey to remove. When he pulled them down over Sam's legs, his hard cock sprang out of its confinement. Joey had to stand up to take off his sleep pants and t-shirt. While he was out of bed, Joey grabbed the supplies from the dresser.

"Let's see what you bought, babe."

When Joey turned back to the bed, he almost swallowed his tongue. All Sam's toned and muscled skin seemed to shine in the moonlight coming in from the nearby window. He lay on his back with his head propped up on a pillow, that sexy smile back and fixed on his face. Joey was doomed. He'd be perpetually horny for the rest of his life. The only piece of fabric that Sam wore was the sling holding his healing arm in place.

Joey walked to the bed and handed Sam the box of condoms and lube before climbing in beside him. Joey ran the palm of his hand across Sam's stomach and chest. His lover's groan surprised him. It was a heady feeling being able to make this big man arch into his touch.

"God, I love it when you touch me. I never want you to stop."

"I don't intend to." Joey was positive about that. Touching Sam had become one of his favorite pastimes. Well, that, and watching him walk around in little to no clothing. The man was hot and all his.

For the first time in his life, Joey felt like he was on solid ground. That the floor underneath him wouldn't crumble away at any moment. It was a freeing feeling he'd never experienced.

Sam set the box down on the bedside table and lifted Joey with his one arm until he was lying directly on top of him. He rubbed against the large hard-on pressing against his thigh. This time Joey dove in for a kiss. He explored Sam's mouth as Sam used his one hand to hold his head in place as he plundered.

Sam lightly bit his bottom lip and then licked away the slight sting. The move only caused Joey to moan even louder. His body felt overheated as chills continued to race up and down his back.

Without breaking their kiss, they rolled over until Sam was now on top, taking over control of Joey's aching body. He didn't want to be in control anymore. He'd always kept a tight rein on himself. He'd had to in order to survive: fighting his disease every step of the way, keeping secrets about his health and his family. He no longer had to carry it all on his own.

Sam braced his forearm above Joey and dove in for another taste like a starving man. Joey wrapped his legs around his lover's muscled thighs and couldn't stop himself from rubbing his straining cock against Sam, trying to find some relief for the ache.

"Touch yourself," Sam ordered. "I want to watch." The gruffness of his voice sent another wave of pleasure straight to Joey's sensitive balls. He'd never masturbated in front of someone before, but with Sam, he had no inhibitions. This was about sharing their bodies with one another, the same as they'd already done with their hearts and souls.

He reached down between his legs as Sam nibbled and sucked his way down Joey's jaw. The moment he took hold of his hard cock, Sam moaned, stopping his exploration to watch him.

Joey pumped his hand up and down, spreading his legs wider with every downward stroke. Sam sucked one of Joey's swollen nipples into his hot, wet mouth, causing his back to bow up off the bed in an attempt to get closer to that talented tongue.

Reaching his other hand down, Joey took hold of Sam's hard cock and began pumping the two in time with one another. Sam's hips began to thrust forward and back, and Joey nearly exploded when he said, "Stroke our cocks together, baby."

He switched his hold to slide both of their cocks in between their joined hands. He began to pant at the feel of all that silky skin. Their mushroomed heads leaked continuously, and he used their precum as lube to help his hands slide more easily.

Sam continued sucking even harder on Joey's nipple while flicking the hard nubbin with his tongue. Electricity shot through Joey's body, and he knew he was close.

"Sam, keep that up, and I'm going to cum," Joey warned before he got too close to the point of no return. He didn't want the pleasure to end so soon.

His love released Joey's sensitive nipple and said, "Grab a condom, baby, and get me ready."

Joey had never been so turned on in his entire life. He reached for the box, pulled a condom out, tore the package open, and slowly rolled it down Sam's cock.

"Now use the lube to get yourself ready for me," Sam instructed. "I prefer to do that, but at the moment, I seem to have run out of arms."

Joey eagerly did as he was asked. Lubing up two fingers, he began loosening his tight muscles, groaning in pleasure with each touch. He lost track of time as he worked his fingers in and out, sliding deeper until he brushed against his prostate, making him gasp.

"That's it, deeper, make room for me, baby." Sam's voice shook, and Joey opened his eyes, unsure when he'd closed them.

Sam's concentration as he watched Joey prepare himself was unwavering. Had anything ever been more erotic? Joey doubted it.

When he was sure he'd stretched enough to take Sam without discomfort, Joey wiped his hand off on the sheets. Sam shifted and lay down on his back. His one arm had to've been straining, and Joey felt stupid for not saying something sooner.

"Come here, baby. Hop up." Sam's voice was rough and deep.

Joey straddled his stomach and leaned forward for another kiss. His cock rubbed between their bodies, leaving a wet trail along Sam's rippled abs and sending another wave of pleasure through him.

"Put me inside of you," Sam instructed. He held the base of his cock as Joey lined the thick mushroom head up with his hole.

The moment Sam slid the end of his cock into him, Joey's world shifted. He placed both of his hands on Sam's broad chest, carding his fingers through his thick black chest hair, and steadied himself.

Sam watched him with such intensity that he couldn't look away. His handsome face was a study in restraint as Joey lowered himself farther, taking more of Sam inside of him. The stretch only intensified Joey's pleasure. All movement felt amplified, and when he bottomed out, Joey could do nothing but moan his need for more.

Leaning forward slightly, he felt the ridges of Sam's cock touching every nerve inside of him. Sam's right hand held on tightly to Joey's hip as he began to slide up and down until he found a rhythm he liked. With each thrust Sam's hips came off the bed to meet him, and it wasn't long before Sam found his prostate and made sure to hit it on every thrust.

"That's it, Joey. Ride me, baby," Sam growled as they picked up speed. Soon Sam took over thrusting in and out of Joey's body as he held on.

One moment he's perched on top of his man, and the next Sam flipped him over and with only his one arm held his body up from crushing Joey. His handsome face was highlighted by the moonlight, allowing Joey to see all the love shining from his dark eyes.

"I love you, Sam." Joey felt like he couldn't say it enough, and as his balls pulled up tight to his body and lightning raced down his spine, he repeated it. "Love you so much."

Sam's face softened and lowered down to kiss him deeply before saying, "You're my everything."

Joey cried out as fire raced from his balls down his cock, exploding in a stream of cum painting both their stomachs. Sam's growl was deep and steady as his hips pumped at a punishing rhythm before thrusting deep one last time and groaning his release to the ceiling. His thick neck was corded with straining muscles, his body held tight, but his face was calm, and his eyes set on Joey.

Joey was gulping down lungfuls of air, too overwhelmed to speak. Neither of them needed their voices to communicate. Between gentle touches and long, lazy kisses, they both knew how the other felt.

***

Joey couldn't have been happier to be back behind the bar in the front lounge. He was only working a few days a week, but it felt wonderful to return. Chitchatting with customers, mixing drinks, and pouring drafts of the finest IPAs in Southern California, he was in his element, and he felt useful again.

Tonight was his second night, and it had been a busy evening. Now, it was late, and most of the patrons had already cleared out by the time Joey got around to restocking the bar. Sam had been upfront several times over the evening to have a quick chat or to simply spend time with him and make sure he was feeling well. It wasn't difficult feeling special with the big guy around.

"Hey, Joey," Mr. Kennedy called. "How about one for the road." His regular was one of the last people in the lounge. The Gates was closing down for the evening in under thirty minutes.

"Of course, sir." Joey pulled a bottle of whiskey down from the shelf behind the bar and brought it over to the counter, along with a tumbler.

"Sure is good to see you're back at work," Mr. Kennedy said. "I was getting worried I'd have to get my old fashioned someplace new from now on."

"I'm happy to be back," Joey agreed. "How's Mrs. Kennedy?" He garnished the drink with a maraschino cherry, walked it over to the end of the bar, and set it down in front of suddenly nervous man.

"Oh, you know, she's angry as always."

He couldn't help but feel for the guy. He looked truly broken up about it. Joey leaned against the bar and said, "I'm sure everything will get better, sir."

"Yes, I believe you're right." Mr. Kennedy's voice had deepened, confusing Joey for a moment until he saw the gun. "Now you have a choice, Joey Venzezo. Either you walk out the front of this building alongside me, or I drag you out while spraying the place with bullets."

His cold eyes were calculating and cruel. How had Joey never seen this side of the man before? "You work for my grandfather?"

"Nope, an independent contractor. Word on the street is that you might be worth over a hundred Gs. I'm sure Bishop will be appreciative when I let him know you've been found."

"You've been planning this from the beginning?"

"No, just lucky, I guess," he sneered as he scanned the area. "Now, come around to the front of the bar so we can get out of here."

Joey looked around, and other than a couple sitting at one of the far tables, they were alone. At this time of night Saint, Max, and Marian would be busy gearing the restaurant down for the day. Sam had offered to help Finn finish organizing the stockroom along with James. He was on his own.

"Do I have to start shooting people?" Kennedy asked, pulling his gun a bit farther out of his jacket.

"No, I'll come with you. Don't hurt anyone." He pictured Sam or one of the crew coming around the corner at any moment and straight into danger. The couple laughing in the corner, the staff, anyone could be hurt. Joey had no choice.

He did as he was asked, the entire time waiting for someone to notice, knowing it would be too late. The tall iron gates that bracketed the main entrance seemed menacing now that he had a gun pointed at his back.

The fresh evening air chilled Joey's sweaty skin, making him shiver. The sidewalk was empty, and he remembered something about bicycle patrols and cruisers watching the building. However, looking around now, he saw no sign of any of them. Not a good time for a break, fellas.

"Keep walking and turn right around the corner. My car's parked down the street."

"So what are you going to do, call my grandfather, make a deal to hand me over to him?"

"That's the plan, kid."

"Is there even a Mrs. Kennedy?" Joey asked. He was trying desperately to stay calm. The last thing he needed was a crisis right now. Stress would thin his veins, making it even harder for his cells to move oxygen around his body.

"Yes, there is, and if I want her to stay that way, I gotta come up with cash fast."

"How did you know it was me they were looking for?" Not as if he were televising the fact.

"Easy. I noticed a few of Bishop's men hanging around the area real interested in your building. After hearing a description of Bishop's poor lost grandson, I couldn't ignore the similarities and the fact that you had the same first name. I thought I'd take a closer look. Final confirmation came when that cop friend of yours showed up. The last word was they shot a cop close to Bishop's grandson. And *voila*, here you are."

"And you expect him to pay you for getting me away from the building?"

"Yep, and a pretty penny it will be." Kennedy chuckled. "The old man has enough money, what's five hundred grand to him."

"I thought you said I was worth one hundred grand?"

"Ya, I did, but I'm sure grandpa money bags won't mind paying a delivery charge."

"You have no idea who you're dealing with." Joey doubted that everything was going to turn out all rosy the way Kennedy believed.

They turned the corner and were about halfway down the block when a dark SUV squealed to a stop ahead of them on the road. At first, Joey thought he was being rescued but soon realized things had gotten infinitely worse. Four men in suits exited the vehicle and headed straight to them.

Kennedy pushed the barrel of his gun against Joey's back but said nothing.

Even the suit couldn't make the first man look any less of a thug. He came to stand in front of him with that same smarmy smile on his face that Joey remembered so well.

"Joey," he said.

"Razor."

"Who's your friend?"

"Oh, you mean my kidnapper. Name's Kennedy."

Razor appraised the man holding a gun on Joey. "We will take him from here."

Kennedy grabbed Joey's arm and painfully pulled him back against him. "I found him for Bishop. I want my reward."

"Reward?"

"Yeah, finder's fee. Five hundred thousand dollars, and you can have him."

"You'll allow us to have Joey?" Razor asked. His voice never changed, but Joey saw all the signs.

Kennedy had no idea who he was messing with, but Joey did.

"Yeah, why do you keep repeating what I'm saying?"

"I wanted to be clear on your demands," Razor said as he pulled out his own gun and pointed at Kennedy's head.

"But I have him. You can't shoot me. I've got a gun pressed against his back. I'll kill him. I swear it. Listen, let's make a deal, I—"

Whatever Kennedy was about to say was lost forever as his body crumpled onto the dirty sidewalk.

Good-bye, Mr. Kennedy.

"Come along, Joey, your grandfather would like a word with you."

"Will there be tea and crumpets? Seriously, Razor, no matter how hard you try, you're still a thug." Joey had no idea where his bravado was coming from, but it was helping him buy some time.

Someone had to notice him missing soon.

He hoped.

Chapter Eleven

"Excuse me."

Sam turned away from the conversation he was having with Saint and James to find a young couple standing only a few feet away. "Can I help you?"

"Yes, we'd like to pay our bill," she explained.

He was confused for a moment. "Where were you sitting?"

"In the lounge. Your bartender left a few minutes ago through the front with an older man. I thought he might be sick, he didn't look well."

Alarms were blaring in Sam's brain. He raced to the front of the building and out onto the sidewalk, James and Saint right behind him. Before he could decide which way to go, he heard a sound that almost brought him to his knees: a gunshot.

They raced down the street, and the moment they rounded the corner, more bullets began to fly. Sam dove behind a parked car as James and Saint managed to make it back around the corner of the building. He peeked out in time to see Joey being thrown into the backseat of the SUV.

Tires squealed, and the kidnappers were down the street by the time he made it out from behind the parked car. He could hear James talking on his phone, no doubt calling for help while Sam ran toward the body left lying on the sidewalk. He recognized the man with a bullet hole in his forehead. The guy had been a regular at the bar.

"Help's on the way," James announced.

Sam's mind was already working on a plan even as his heart felt like it was being squeezed in a vise. He was of no use to Joey if he lost it. Sam needed to be at the top of his game, injured arm or not, to get his love back, and they would get Joey back. He would make Bishop regret ever looking for his grandson.

***

Joey had thought he'd never see this room again, or rather had prayed not to. The walls of polished wood shone as brightly as the dozen or so glass eyes staring down at him. He'd never understood trophy hunting. Why would anyone want to kill these beautiful and endangered animals?

Well, considering whose house he was now standing in, Joey understood. A predator would always be a predator, and his grandfather had the bloodlust to prove it. From elephant to lion, and a multitude of rare animals in between, heads were hung on the walls, or posed behind glass, stuffed and standing upright on his grandfather's study floor. Horns, feet, and tusks adorned the polished shelves, while animal pelts covered the backs of the couch and a chair.

Gruesome had always been the way Joey had thought about this room back to the day he could first remembered being here. Grandad had always chosen to dole out his punishments in this room. The asshole knew how much the dead animals bothered him, adding a morbid twist to each imagined transgression Joey had ever made.

He tried to keep Sam in the forefront of his thoughts, to be strong. Joey knew, without a doubt, his man would find him. Joey had to hold out until they got here.

"I see things don't change," a gruff voice said from behind him, sending cold chills through his body. "You still look at my prizes with disgust."

"Hello, Grandfather." Calm, stay calm.

"Welcome home, Joey. Unfortunately for you, it won't be a long stay."

Joey figured they might as well get this over with; the anticipation was doing shit for his nerves. "What do you want?"

Bishop rounded his desk, giving Joey the first look he'd had of the man from his nightmares in nineteen years. Time hadn't been kind to his grandfather. His once dark wavy hair had thinned and turned gray, and his stomach bulged out from between his suit jacket. Deep wrinkles seemed to highlight his scar even more than before, giving him an almost jack-o-lantern look. Joey had given him that scar the last time his grandfather ever hit his mom. The one and only time he'd ever touched one of his grandfather's prizes. Joey hadn't known how much damage an antelope horn could do.

However, one thing remained: that psychotic look in the old man's eyes. The look that warned you not to turn your back to him, or get too close because you could never be sure what he'd do. Bishop had proven how volatile he could be on many occasions. Joey remembered the one time a man had dared to honk his horn at them in traffic.

Dear old grandad had gotten out of the limousine, smashed the driver's window out of the other car, and pulled the man out in front of his wife and children. Then proceeded to beat him with a pair of brass knuckles and left him in a pool of his own blood on the roadway. Joey had been eight.

"I want you to save my son," Bishop said, and he looked serious.

"Excuse me, how?" He had nothing and wasn't a doctor.

"He needs a kidney transplant, or he will die."

Joey could never in a million years have guessed that's what his grandfather brought him back here to do. "I don't think I can donate a kidney with my disease." The words even sounded weird, coming out of his mouth.

He wanted him to donate one of his kidneys to save Luca? If that's genuinely what he'd wanted all along, why bother with all the guns and violence? *He could have simply asked me.*

A knock on the study door interrupted whatever his grandfather was about to say. "Come in."

The door opened, and two men in lab coats came walking in carrying what looked like a fishing tackle box. This couldn't be good. Razor and a few of his men followed them in and surrounded Joey.

"We need a sample of your blood," Bishop explained. "We can either do this the hard way, or you can sit down and allow the doctors to take your blood."

Okay, this was going a bit far. He hadn't agreed to the donation, but if Joey fought, he'd likely end up in the middle of a pain crisis before Sam could save him.

Razor looked ready to take him down, so he calmly sat in the chair behind him and rolled up his sleeve. The goon didn't look happy, but Joey had to play along for as long as he could, but that didn't include surgery.

Bishop looked at him appraisingly. "I see you've gained some sense over the years."

One of the doctors knelt down beside him and began wrapping a rubber tourniquet around his left arm.

"You may go," Bishop ordered Razor and his men to leave, not amusing Razor in the least. However, they left, but Joey knew that wouldn't be the end of it.

He cringed when the needle broke his skin and watched as his dysfunctional blood flowed into one vile after another. Joey was getting worried after the sixth vial, but fortunately, there wasn't a seventh. They slapped a bandage on him and left the room without either of them saying a word or looking him in the eyes.

"We'll have the results in a few hours. Until then, you will stay in your old bedroom," Bishop announced, and the study doors flew open once again. "Take him away."

Razor grabbed his right arm and dragged Joey out of the chair. Before he had a chance to say another word, they walked him down the long marble-tiled hall. Joey remembered how hard marble could be if you landed on it with anything other than your feet. Instead of taking the stairs, they headed for the elevator.

Shit. The two of them alone in an elevator didn't sound promising for Joey's continued ability to stand. Razor's grin confirmed it wasn't.

"Razor," a man called from behind them. "The boss wants to see you."

His grip tightened around Joey's upper arm, making him wince in pain. "I'll be back down in a couple minutes."

"Bishop said now. I can take him."

He growled and looked down at Joey. "I'll be sure to stop by later tonight," he said before pushing him toward the second man.

As Razor stormed off, Joey was again dragged toward the elevator. Once in the tiny box, he expected to be slapped around a little for fun, as they liked to call it, but the man didn't move. The bell dinged for the third floor, and the doors opened. It felt surreal to be standing in this hallway once again.

The door to his mother's old bedroom stood open on the right as they walked by, and Joey could make out a few of his mother's belongings where they'd been left almost two decades ago. The next was *Nonna*'s room, and Joey's heart ached that he never had a chance to say good-bye to her. She had loved him. There had never been a doubt.

Eventually, they made it to his room at the end of the hall. The thug opened the door and shoved him in. Joey heard the lock click as he was transported back in time. Everything in his room had been left exactly as he remembered it. His single bed was still made, and his favorite die-cast car sat waiting on a dusty track.

Joey walked over to the closet and looked inside. Sure enough, the clothing he wore before they'd left still hung on the wooden rod. Holy shit, he was having a hard time staying calm. In different circumstances, in a world where his grandfather loved him, this would be sweet and touching. In the real world, where Joey had been hated and persecuted, this was some seriously messed-up shit.

Everywhere he looked were memories of his boyhood self. It was equal parts soothing to remember his mom and *Nonna*, and terrifying to remember what carried on behind the walls of this house on the hill.

His stress level was picking up by leaps and bounds, so Joey concentrated on Sam. Being back in Sam's arms, playing his racing games, making love, all helped to calm him. He could feel the pain increasing in his stomach, never a good sign.

Joey wasn't an idiot, not by a long shot when it came to his grandfather. If Bishop wanted his kidney, nothing Joey had to say would make a difference. He even doubted that they intended for him to live through the surgery.

There was only one thing he could do: escape.

Joey walked over to the small bookcase and desk he'd spent many a night sitting at when he hadn't been allowed to lie in his bed. He prayed that his grandfather hadn't found his secret. Would it even be there after all these years? After one final listen to make sure no one was coming down the hallway, Joey pulled the bookcase a few inches back from the wall and almost cried when he saw it was still there.

It could have been a cave full of diamonds for how happy he was at the sight of the hole he had dug into the plastered wall. When he was a child, he'd often been locked in his room at his grandfather's will. Over time, Joey found his own way out when he was fortunate enough to watch a plumber who'd been working on pipes in the walls around the mansion. That's when he noticed that the crawl spaces were big enough for him to easily walk along. A bonus feature of an old house built in the glitz and glam of Hollywood's heyday, strange building codes, and eccentric owners.

Of course, Joey wasn't as small as he'd been when he first began chiseling away at the plaster. Though, for the first time in his life, his small stature would prove to be a gift. He took one last look around his bedroom that had been frozen in time, and crawled through the hole, pulling the bookcase back into place behind him.

***

Sam stood in the briefing room, securing his bulletproof vest into place before holstering his gun. Busted arm or not, he was going in after Joey. He would never leave his man's safety in someone else's hands. The team consisted of SWAT units, uniformed officers, and undercover officers. James and Miguel had already staked out the Venzezo estate and had been keeping them up to date on the activity inside the compound.

Ross and the captain were running the show, and Sam's only mission was to find his love and protect him until he could get him out of the house. There was no doubt he would bring Joey back and rain hell down on anyone who tried to stop him.

"Everyone has their orders. Make sure to stay in your teams and clear one room at a time. We don't need anyone caught in the crossfire. We're hoping that Bishop and his people won't think we could muster a team this quickly. We have the element of surprise on our side. We should reach the estate gates by three. Team one will take the north gate, while team two goes in from the east." Captain Meyers pointed out each position on the map hanging on the back wall. He was a solid leader, younger than most captains on the force, but passionate and fair. Sam had respect for him and his ability to assess a situation and act accordingly.

Sam had his head in the game, reliable and sure of his ability. Joey needed the best out of him, and he would get it.

An officer came walking in through the conference room door and up to the captain and Ross. They said a few words before the detective looked over at him and motioned for Sam to follow him out into the hall. He walked out of the room to find a person he never expected to see anywhere near here leaning against the wall.

"Brad, what are you doing here?" Sam asked.

The young man stood and straightened his back. "I came to help you get Joey out of Bishop's house."

Sam looked over at Ross and the captain for clarification, but both looked as confused as he was.

"How do you know any of this happened?" Ross asked. "It's been less than two hours since Joey was taken."

"News travels fast on the street. You guys should know that better than anyone."

"Why do you think you can help us?" Sam asked, still confused by Brad's offer.

"I know how to get in without setting off the alarms."

"You're going to have to be a little more forthcoming than that, Brad," Captain Meyers said before crossing his arms. "Why would you help us, and how would you know how to get into that estate?"

Brad became nervous but never wavered from looking Meyers in the eyes. "I used to be a burglar, a really good one."

"Used to be?" Meyers asked.

"I haven't returned to the life in over two years." Brad took a deep breath. "I know several ways of moving around this city and through some prominent homes without being seen."

"You do realize you're standing in a police station?" Ross asked.

"Oh, was that what those signs said all over the front of the building?" Brad remarked with a withering look that made the captain grin. "Of course I do. Like I said, I'm no longer in the business. I make my money the honest way now."

"Why do you want to help us get to Joey?" Sam asked because there was always a chance that Brad was leading them straight into a trap.

Brad's eyes seemed to soften. "The small dude never hurt anyone. He's kind and always willing to help out or listen to me ramble on about one thing or another. I could tell Joey had concerns about me in the beginning, you know, some habits are hard to break. He watched me like a hawk, but he gave me a chance. Shit, he never complains even though he's sick himself."

"How did you know that?" Sam asked because that information wasn't public knowledge.

"I've got eyes, so I asked him. Joey didn't tell me what was wrong, but he confirmed he was fighting something. It doesn't matter. He doesn't deserve whatever that fucked-up asshole has planned for him, and if I can help, I will."

Sam looked at the young man closely. "Aren't you afraid by telling us this you'll get yourself in trouble and fired from your job?" Seriously, who comes out and tells a building full of cops you're some kind of master thief?

"Of course I am, but it won't stop me from doing the right thing by Joey."

He looked over at the captain. "I believe him, sir."

"So do I," Ross seconded.

"Okay, Brad, let's hear what you've got," Captain Meyers said while uncrossing his arms.

Sam's phone beeped, indicating he had a text message. While Brad carried on with his explanation, he reached into one of the pockets on his vest and pulled out his phone. When he saw the message on the screen and who it was from, he almost dropped to the floor in relief.

"Joey?"

Chapter Twelve

He looked down at the bright screen on the cell phone Sam had given him. Joey had forgotten entirely that he'd put it in his pocket after turning it on silent before work. Razor and his goons had been so confident in their ability to handle Joey that they hadn't even bothered checking him for anything. Their oversight was his gain.

After he'd crawled back in between the walls, he quickly got turned around. It had been a lifetime since he'd crawled along the eighteen-inch gaps between the exterior and interior walls. After about ten minutes, he finally found a few signs he'd left along the way when he'd been a child. A couple toy cars and an old comic book, belongings he'd treasured and wanted to hide away from his grandfather so they wouldn't be destroyed.

When Joey had bent over to pick up a die-cast car, he felt his cell phone jam him in his leg. He couldn't believe his luck when he pulled it out and saw that it still had reception. He turned on the light on his phone and made his way deeper into the walls. It wasn't until Joey was sure he'd left a considerable distance between himself and his old bedroom that he finally stopped to crouch down and send a message.

God, he hoped Sam had his cell phone on him. After ensuring that his phone was still on silent, he tapped out his SOS.

Sam, I'm locked in my grandfather's house.

Please, please, please, let him see it. Joey sat staring at the screen for what felt like an eternity before receiving a reply.

Joey, I need to confirm this is truly you. What's my favorite pastime?

Joey hadn't even thought of that. His grandfather could have found his phone and was using it as a trap to find out what the police had planned. How Bishop ever thought he could kidnap him without someone noticing and coming after him was a mystery. Then it struck him: up until a few months ago, no one would have noticed if Joey had gone missing.

Playing racing games on the television in your boxers with me.

He slipped in the last part, so there would be no doubt. Who else would know about the boxers, and the "with me" was because he could. As he waited for a reply, Joey decided his best plan would be to make his way up to the attic as he used to do. From there, he'd figure out his next steps.

Are you hurt?

Joey quickly typed.

No. Got out of my old room and hiding. Going to head for the attic. I don't think they know I'm missing yet. My grandfather wants my kidney for his son, and he doesn't care how he gets it.

Joey hoped he went unnoticed for as long as possible. They'd tear the house apart looking for him if they knew he'd escaped.

We're on our way to get you. Stay hidden, and I'll find you.

That sounded perfect to Joey. The sooner he got out of this house of horrors, the better.

Okay, I'll be in the attic. I love you, Sam.

Joey wanted to take the opportunity to repeat those words in case he didn't have another chance. He didn't fool himself into not believing that if Razor and his men ever found him, that he'd never see the light of day ever again.

I love you, Joey. I'm coming for you.

He couldn't help but smile even though he was stuck in the dusty walls of a madman's house. If anyone could get him out of this alive, it would be Sam.

Joey turned his camera's flashlight up and began the climb. Long ago, he'd figured out that the original builder had left a gap between the fireplace and the floorboards where the third floor and the attic met. It wasn't much of a space, but he hoped it was enough for him to squeeze through.

With every step, stretch, twist, and pull, Joey felt his body straining to keep up. His joints were beginning to ache, and his head was throbbing, but he pushed harder then he'd ever done before. He refused to die in the one place he'd been running from his entire life.

Halfway up, Joey had to take a break. His body didn't approve of wall climbing. He'd managed to scrape his back and rip his shirt on a nail sticking out of the walls. The lathes underneath the plaster walls were a minefield of sharp, pointy things ready to cause him pain and inevitably an infection considering the dusty, cobwebbed space. This had sure been a hell of a lot easier when he was a kid.

Joey used the flashlight sparingly to cut through the inky darkness, not wanting to wear out what was left of his battery. With only the occasional beam of light coming through old vents, if he didn't monitor how much battery he had left, Joey would soon find himself banging around in the dark. That was a terrifying idea.

He had no idea how long he'd been climbing through the walls, but he knew he was close to his destination when the sound he had been dreading rang through the walls.

"Find him." His grandfather's voice echoed around Joey. He'd always had the ability to make his voice travel across the house.

His disappearance was no longer a secret, and the alarms had begun sounding. There was no doubt in Joey's mind that Razor had come back to pay him a visit only to find the room empty. He couldn't help but feel a tiny bit of satisfaction about disappointing the bastard.

The sound of people racing through the halls matched his own heartbeat. Now that they knew he was gone, the timer had been set on how much time he had left before they found him.

Joey kept moving, and when he'd almost reached the attic floorboards, he heard voices coming from above him.

"I won't be the one to tell him that Luca has died. I'm leaving," an angry voice announced. "You can stick around here and see what happens when he finds out."

Shit, there's no reason to keep me alive now.

The realization felt like the final nail in his coffin.

Please hurry, Sam, I'm running out of time.

***

Sam followed the former burglar across the manicured lawn and past the trimmed hedges until they were only a couple hundred yards from Bishop's mansion. Crime apparently paid well by the looks of this place. It gutted him knowing his Joey was trapped inside that monstrosity, but he swore it wouldn't be for much longer.

No one wanted a civilian involved in any possible firefight. However, Brad explained that he couldn't adequately describe the path he'd followed to get in without risking them being found out before the other teams stormed the estate, which made it imperative that Brad came along.

At first, it had been a straight shot over a few hills behind the property, making Sam wonder when the difficult part would begin. He didn't have to wait long. Before they'd even reached the edge of the crime boss's property, they came upon two sets of security sensors hidden in the long grasses ready to alert Bishop to any movement.

With a skill Sam hadn't had the opportunity to ever see in person, Brad placed at least a dozen small receivers in strategic positions as he made a path through the trap for their small group to pass. All this was done with only the light of the moon to help him see what he was doing. Sam, Ross, and the captain exchanged a few shocked and impressed looks, while Brad quickly disarmed every security measure they'd come across. How had this guy stayed under police radar?

As if sensing this unasked question, Brad whispered, "I'd only steal from known criminals. They were less likely to call you guys after a break-in." Oddly, that made sense. They wouldn't want the police poking around their homes looking for evidence.

Sam could see figures moving around behind the drape-covered windows. There looked to be a lot of action for three in the morning.

"Something's up," Ross said as he scanned the area.

"They must have found out Joey is missing," Sam replied. "We have to hurry and get in there before they have a chance to find him."

"Let's move," Captain Meyers said as he pulled out his service revolver.

Sam lifted his own gun, and they all dashed for the side of the house. He had to admit it was a bit more complicated with only one functioning arm. They were led to an old cellar door, making Sam think it couldn't be this easy. Sure enough, Brad reached around the concrete casing and produced a key.

At their combined stares, Brad explained, "The gardener is forgetful. He leaves a key hidden so that he can access his tools every morning."

How long had he been casing this house? If anything, he was thorough. Sam imagined if the bartender had wanted to, he'd have already cleaned Saint out. That he hadn't had to be a step in the right direction. He hoped.

They could hear a man yelling, and his words confirmed his suspicions. "Find him."

Brad unlocked the door and disappeared into the darkness of the cellar. A few seconds later, he returned and waved them forward. Once they were all inside, they cleared the room and then waited for the signal.

Every second Sam waited only increased his anxiety, knowing at any moment they could find Joey. He needed to get inside and stop them before it was too late.

It didn't take long before the security alarms started sounding, indicating the SWAT teams had breached the gates of the estate. The sound of people running to the front of the house assured their entrance would go unnoticed for at least a few seconds, giving them enough time to make it to the staircase.

Brad stood by the door leading into the house, waiting for the word to move. He wasn't armed, but his shadow, the captain, was: he stood only a foot away. Gunfire broke out, and their team rushed from the cellar and into an expansive kitchen. Thankfully, it was empty. They began spreading out to cover all the entrances leading in while he, Brad, and the captain headed for the back stairwell that Sam assumed was for the staff.

They were going by reconnaissance and old city building records, but so far, every part of the house was as the drawings said they'd be. It was fortunate that no one had done any significant renovations over the last twenty-five years.

The three made their way up one floor at a time. The commotion downstairs was raging on as they made it to the second floor. They turned the corner and found themselves face to face with a man in a white coat racing down the stairs. Brad pushed them both out of the way as the man shot off a few rounds in their direction.

Sam quickly recovered and returned fire, hitting their attacker in the center of his chest. He turned to check on the other two to find Captain Meyers applying a tourniquet made out of his torn shirt to Brad's arm. Two more officers came running up the stairs at the sound of the gunfire.

"It's nothing, keep going. Joey's only two floors up," Brad said as he tried to brush away the captain's attempts at further help. "I'll stay with these two officers."

Sam was already heading down the hallway to the second set of stairs when Captain Meyers caught up with him.

Sam wasn't stopping until he held Joey safe in his arms again.

Chapter Thirteen

Joey heard one of the men leave, followed shortly after by the second. He wondered what they had been doing in the attic in the first place. He pushed himself high enough to pop his head out and take a look around before climbing from his hiding spot and saw no one.

As quietly as possible, he wiggled his way out from between the floorboards and the back of the freestanding brick fireplace. There were lights on, but they'd been dimmed, and as Joey inched his way around to the front, he heard gunfire break out downstairs and saw flashing lights through the attic windows.

Sam was here. He'd come for him.

Joey's relief was short-lived, though, when he saw what was on the other side of the fireplace. The attic he remembered with its boxes and old furniture was gone, and in its place, a medical bay any hospital would be proud to call their own. In the center of all the machines was a bed with a lone figure lying on it.

This had to be his uncle, Luca. Why would his grandfather move all this up here into the attic? It had to be easier to care for him on the main level of the house instead of hiding him away up here. Why would he want to have Luca so far away?

The machines around the bed were silent, and the figure on the bed wasn't breathing. This was what the doctors had run from. Joey could understand. He doubted his grandfather would have listened to reason. He could hear more shots being fired at the front of the house, but all of Joey's attention was drawn to the bed. He'd had an uncle and never known it. Had he been more like his sister, Joey's mom, or like his father, Bishop? Questions Joey would never have answers to.

The figure on the bed was young, maybe eighteen, and Joey's heart went out to him. Even though his grandfather had intended to use him for spare parts, had Joey known he had an uncle, and things had been different, who knew what might have happened? Looking at his dead uncle, Joey thought, another young life had been cut short.

"Get away from him." His grandfather's voice echoed through the attic.

Joey slowly stepped away from the bed and turned around to face the man who wanted to see him dead. For the first time in his life, he saw his grandfather disheveled. His suit coat was gone, and his gray hair was standing on end as if he'd run his fingers through it more than a few times.

Bishop looked from the machines and down to his son. "What have you done?"

"This wasn't me. The doctors ran out of here after Luca passed away. I found him like this," Joey explained, and for some unknown reason, he felt he needed to follow it up with. "I'm sorry."

When Bishop looked back up at him, Joey expected to see sadness but found only hate. "You're sorry. Between the two of you, I couldn't even get one decent heir to the Venzezo dynasty."

Joey's picture of the situation was getting clearer all the time. "You didn't love him as your son, only a commodity to be used to extend your family line. Wow, you're more fucked up than I ever imagined." He didn't bother censoring his words around his grandfather anymore. This was the final chapter of their story. One of them wouldn't be leaving this room, and as his grandfather raised his gun, Joey suspected it wouldn't be him.

"Fucked up. You have no idea." Bishop's laughter led Joey to believe his grandfather had finally lost his mind. "Haven't you ever wondered who or where your father is?"

"Let me guess: you killed him. Cut him into little pieces and fed him to the fishes." Joey refused to be his victim any longer. "Or better yet, you chained him in your cellar, and he's still down there waiting for me." Though he hated all those scenarios, Joey wouldn't allow his grandfather to see it.

Instead of being shocked as Joey had hoped, his grandfather smiled even wider. "I like the way you think. More like your old man than I thought."

"What the hell do you mean by that?"

"As a parting gift, I'll tell you who he is before I kill you."

"Why would I believe anything you say?"

"Choose to believe me or not, but in your last few seconds of life, know that the blood of a man you despise runs through your veins. Razor."

Joey didn't even have a chance to respond before another voice joined the conversation. "You told me Lillian was with another man." Razor's voice was even colder than Joey had ever heard it before.

"You and my mom?" Joey asked.

"He was a different man back then, weren't you, Razor? All noble and shit." Bishop laughed even harder. "If I'd told you the truth, you would have been useless to me."

Joey was having a hard time wrapping his brain around what he was hearing, but that didn't matter when his grandfather pointed the gun at his head. "You've been a disappointment to me long before your birth. Be sure to give my best to your mother."

Joey closed his eyes. He didn't want to see his grandfather pull the trigger. A single shot sounded. It took him a few seconds to realize that he hadn't been hit. His eyes flew open to find his grandfather lying on the attic floor with Razor standing over the body, gun in hand. He wasn't sure what to do but felt a whole lot better once Razor lowered his weapon.

"I didn't know. I thought you were someone else's son," Razor explained, as if that fixed everything.

No doubt, Joey would need therapy after this one. The pain in his stomach was getting much worse. The man who had made his life hell, doled out punishments, and derived pleasure from Joey's tears was his biological father. Dear old Grandad got the last laugh after all.

"LAPD, drop the gun," Sam ordered from the attic door.

Razor didn't even hesitate, and his gun fell to the floor. Joey ran across the room and to Sam's side.

"Are you hurt?" Sam asked while another officer rushed in and cuffed Razor.

"Not from them, but my stomach and joints are sore, and I have a blinding headache. I don't want another pain crisis."

Once they had Razor subdued, Sam holstered his gun and wrapped his arm around Joey and headed for the door. His love knew precisely what he needed, and that was to get as far away from this place as possible.

He barely registered his feet touching the stairs before Joey realized they were walking out of the front door and straight to a waiting vehicle. The entire ride home he spent buried against Sam's chest as his love held him tight.

"It's all over, honey," Sam crooned. "You'll never have to worry about any of them ever again."

Joey wished that were true.

"The man you saved me from, his name is Razor, one of my grandfather's men, and according to him, my father." Joey couldn't even believe he was saying those words. "He shot Bishop when he found out. What if he is? The evil in him could run through me."

Sam held him tight and said, "There's no chance of that happening ever. You're your mother's son, and I believe nurture over nature supersedes everything, especially in your case. You could never be evil, Joey."

Joey prayed Sam was right. For now, he had to let it go, or the knowledge was going to make him sick. What he needed right now was a hot shower to wash away every last remnant of his grandfather, Razor, and that house.

***

Sam held his love as tight as he could without hurting him. It would be a long time before he felt calm enough to let Joey go. When he was running up the stairs and heard the gunshot from the attic, he lost it, thinking the worse. He never wanted to go through that again.

With all the shit going on around him, Sam was surprised Joey wasn't already in the middle of a crisis brought on by the stress. As promised, Sam had researched sickle cell disease exhaustively and understood that his love's bloodstream might be having a hard time providing enough oxygen to his entire body. Sam would get him home where he could take care of Joey because making sure he was comfortable was mission one. He didn't think a visit to the hospital would be good for the already traumatized man.

Miguel and James sat in the front of the vehicle, and they were heading straight for The Gates. Captain Meyers knew where to find them when he needed a debriefing and statement. There was no way in hell Sam would make Joey wait around there to give one.

When they pulled up to the back of the building, The Gates crew was waiting for them.

"We're home, honey," Sam said, causing Joey to look up. "I'll have you cleaned up and resting in no time."

Joey didn't answer, no doubt still running the day's events through his mind. If Bishop wasn't already dead, Sam would have made sure of it himself. The man's reign of terror had known no bounds, and even in death, he was still fucking with his grandson.

The whole issue about Razor could wait. The guy would be easy to find cooling his heels in a jail cell. Of course, they wouldn't take Bishop's word as truth, and when or if Joey wanted to know the truth, they'd cross that bridge together.

Hours later, Joey was cuddled into bed beside Sam, who had treated all Joey's cuts and scrapes after having a hot shower. Marian had brought him a plate of food in case Joey was hungry.

The sun was beginning to rise by the time they'd settled in, but Sam was still wired from the events of the last eight hours. He'd believed Joey was asleep until he spoke.

"It doesn't matter."

"What doesn't matter, honey?"

"Who my father is," Joey said. "You're right. I am my mother's son, and no one else's. I won't tarnish her memory because of one evil old man's words."

"By everything you've told me, your mother was a remarkable woman. She loved you very much."

"She did," Joey confirmed. "I remember once…"

For the next thirty minutes, Joey regaled him with story after story about his mother and their adventures, until he eventually fell asleep. Sam lay there long after Joey drifted off, listening to his breathing even out and formulating a plan to help Joey move on from this.

He hoped what he was considering doing was the right thing.

Chapter Fourteen

It had been weeks since his grandfather was killed, and Joey had had a harder time than he'd expected moving on from it. Word on the street said that the Venzezo family hold on LA was over, and new factions had already divided the leftovers, which was a fitting end to his grandfather's legacy. Razor would be sitting in jail to await his trial and thankfully hadn't attempted to contact him.

Joey stood behind his bar, one of his happiest places other than being with Sam, who had been in a meeting with Saint for the better part of the last hour. He couldn't help but wonder what was going on, but knew Sam would tell him since they had no more secrets between them.

It was weird, but he'd still catch himself staring at the far end of the bar and wondering what Mrs. Kennedy was doing right now. Was she sad her husband was gone, or happy to finally be free of him? The whole thing reinforced the fact that you never really knew someone. A friend could actually be your worst enemy.

He was the first to admit he'd been in a funk since that day, and Joey wasn't sure how to pull himself out of it. A chapter of his life he'd thought closed had been blown open in spectacular fashion, and he felt like he was still trying to pick up the pieces.

Sam had been supportive through it all, and Joey wasn't sure what he would have done without him.

As if speaking of the man made him appear, Sam and Brad came walking into the lounge. He'd been shocked when he learned what Brad had done for him, but it made his behavior much more understandable. Saint hadn't fired him, stating he could have cleaned him out already if he'd wanted to, and Captain Meyers hadn't arrested him. According to Sam, Brad admitted to his prior life, but it'd been vague, and they had no evidence of its veracity or cases tied to anyone who looked like Brad.

"Hey, Joey," Brad said. "I'm here to take over for you."

"For me? But I have two more hours of my shift left."

"Your man wants a word with you." Brad laughed as if that were code for sexy times and wiggled his eyebrows accordingly. "I'm pretty sure you're going to need the rest of the day off."

Joey couldn't help but laugh. "Oh, do you?"

Sam stood on the other side of the bar. He looked happy, but there was something else lurking in those dark brown eyes. "Hey, honey, I have something I'd like you to see."

Curiosity piqued, Joey went around the bar and took Sam's outstretched hand. Instead of leading Joey to the hub, they walked over to the bank of elevators over on the opposite side of the building. He'd never used these elevators before. They required a key to access.

They got on, and Sam wrapped his arm around Joey and pulled him close. "I love you."

"I love you too," Joey replied. "Is everything okay?" Sam was acting odd.

"Yeah, Nothing's wrong, love. I'd like your opinion on something."

Joey's curiosity was through the roof, but he stopped himself from asking any more questions when Sam bent down to kiss him deeply. All thought fled at the feel of Sam's soft lips against his own.

The elevator dinged, and the doors slid open, but his love didn't break the kiss. As the doors began to close, he shot his hand out to stop them and finished thoroughly exploring Joey's mouth. When they broke apart, his head spun a little.

"Whatever I did to deserve that, tell me, so I can do it again," Joey teased while hugging himself closer to Sam.

"There's nothing for you to do again. It's you exactly as you are," Sam said as he took Joey's hand and continued down the hall.

Max's construction crew had already moved on to the third floor of the building and finished the four condo units on this floor. Joey hadn't seen any of them, but he heard a few of the workers commenting about how happy they were with the way they'd turned out.

Sam stopped outside a door with the number one carved into a gold plate in the center. He unlocked the door and ushered Joey into what had to be one of the best condos in DTLA. Open ceilings showcased shiny ductwork and hanging lights, while the old brickwork had been restored and took a prominent place as the entire back wall. The original casement windows had been restored and replaced, allowing the California sunshine to flood in.

The space was wide open and airy. The stunning blue-tiled backsplash worked well with the stainless steel appliances in the large kitchen. Past the rectangular island, he could see into a space that made up a roomy living room. Of course, the rooms were still empty, but Joey could imagine it as if the pieces of furniture were there.

The light hardwood floors gleamed and seemed to be throughout the unit. To his left stood a hallway leading to a good-sized bathroom and bedroom. To his right was the door leading to the master bedroom and en suite, which were substantially larger than the other bedroom.

He couldn't help but imagine these rooms full of furniture with pops of color. Ideas and pictures from his mother's decorating magazines raced through his head. The place was a blank canvas waiting for someone to bring it to life. The structure and finishes were top-notch. He wouldn't change a thing about them. Decorating was where someone could really put their stamp on the place.

"What do you think?" Sam asked. Up until now, he'd followed Joey around in silence.

"I think it's stunning. I'd heard good things about Connor Construction, and Max's company certainly lived up to it. Someone's going to love this place."

"Apparently, the owners already do."

"It's sold?"

"Yeah. To us."

Joey opened his mouth, but no words came out. Sam closed the distance between them and got down on one knee. He pulled a gold band from his pocket and held it out to him.

"Marry me," Sam said in his upfront and straight-to-the-point manner. No flowery words, simply love.

"Yes, I will marry you, Sam. I've never wanted anything more."

As Sam slid the gold band onto his finger, Joey now understood what his mom had always told him. Love has the power to change someone's life, but real love showed you that the life you have is worth living.

ABOUT THE AUTHOR

M. Tasia lives in a small town in Ontario, Canada. She's a member of the Romance Writers of America, and its Rainbow Romance Writers and Toronto Romance Writers chapters. Michelle is a dedicated people-watcher, lover of romance novels, '80s rock, and happy endings. Also, she's the mother of two wonderful girls, wife to a great husband, and new grandmother, as well as servant to two spoiled furry children who don't seem to realize that they're actually cats.

Michelle writes contemporary and paranormal romance, and she believes love should be celebrated. After all, everybody needs a little romance, excitement, intrigue, and passion in their lives.

Connect with Michelle:

mtasiabooks.com

facebook.com/mtasiabooks

twitter.com/mtasiaauthor

instagram.com/m.tasia.author/

www.BOROUGHSPUBLISHINGGROUP.com

If you enjoyed this book, please write a review. Our authors appreciate the feedback, and it helps future readers find books they love. We welcome your comments and invite you to send them to info@boroughspublishinggroup.com. Follow us on Facebook, Twitter and Instagram, and be sure to sign up for our newsletter for surprises and new releases from your favorite authors.

Are you an aspiring writer? Check out www.boroughspublishinggroup.com/submit and see if we can help you make your dreams come true.